THE EARLY SHORT FICTION OF EDITH WHARTON

BY

EDITH WHARTON

A TEN-VOLUME COLLECTION
VOLUME ONE

British Library Cataloguing-in-Publication Data
A catalogue record for this book is available from the
British Library

CONTENTS

CONTENTS

Edith Wharton

Edith Wharton was born in New York City in 1862. Her family were extremely wealthy, and during her youth she was provided private tuition and travelled extensively in Europe. A voracious reader, Wharton studied literature, philosophy, science, and art, and began to write poetry and short fiction. In 1885, aged 23, Edith married a banker, Edward Robbins, and for the next few years they travelled extensively together. Living near Central Park in New York, Wharton's first poems were published in *Scribner's Magazine*. In 1891, the same publication printed the first of her many short stories, titled 'Mrs. Manstey's View'. Over the next four decades, they – along with other well-established American publications such as *Atlantic Monthly, Century Magazine, Harper's* and *Lippincott's* – regularly published her work.

A lifelong keen architect, in 1902 Wharton designed and built her home, The Mount, in Lenox, Massachusetts. It was while living here that she wrote many of her works, including the 1905 novel *The House of Mirth*, which was that year's bestseller, and is now considered a classic of American literary Naturalism. In the period leading up to the First World War, Wharton wrote prolifically, and in 1921 she received the Pulitzer Prize – the first ever woman to do so – for her novel *The Age of Innocence*. Like much of her work, the novel examines the tension between societal pressures and the pursuit of genuine happiness, and includes careful use of dramatic irony.

Edith Wharton died of a stroke in 1937, aged 75. In addition to her novels, she is remembered for her short fiction, especially her excellent ghost stories.

KERFOL

As first published in Scribner's Magazine, March 1916

CHAPTER I

"You ought to buy it," said my host; "it's just the place for a solitary-minded devil like you. And it would be rather worth while to own the most romantic house in Brittany. The present people are dead broke, and it's going for a song—you ought to buy it."

It was not with the least idea of living up to the character my friend Lanrivain ascribed to me (as a matter of fact, under my unsociable exterior I have always had secret yearnings for domesticity) that I took his hint one autumn afternoon and went to Kerfol. My friend was motoring over to Quimper on business: he dropped me on the way, at a cross-road on a heath, and said: "First turn to the right and second to the left. Then straight ahead till you see an avenue. If you meet any peasants, don't ask your way. They don't understand French, and they would pretend they did and mix you up. I'll be back for you here by sunset—and don't forget the tombs in the chapel."

I followed Lanrivain's directions with the hesitation

occasioned by the usual difficulty of remembering whether he had said the first turn to the right and second to the left, or the contrary. If I had met a peasant I should certainly have asked, and probably been sent astray; but I had the desert landscape to myself, and so stumbled on the right turn and walked on across the heath till I came to an avenue. It was so unlike any other avenue I have ever seen that I instantly knew it must be THE avenue. The grey-trunked trees sprang up straight to a great height and then interwove their pale-grey branches in a long tunnel through which the autumn light fell faintly. I know most trees by name, but I haven't to this day been able to decide what those trees were. They had the tall curve of elms, the tenuity of poplars, the ashen colour of olives under a rainy sky; and they stretched ahead of me for half a mile or more without a break in their arch. If ever I saw an avenue that unmistakably led to something, it was the avenue at Kerfol. My heart beat a little as I began to walk down it.

Presently the trees ended and I came to a fortified gate in a long wall. Between me and the wall was an open space of grass, with other grey avenues radiating from it. Behind the wall were tall slate roofs mossed with silver, a chapel belfry, the top of a keep. A moat filled with wild shrubs and brambles surrounded the place; the drawbridge had been replaced by a stone arch, and the portcullis by an iron gate. I stood for a long time on the hither side of the moat, gazing about me, and letting the influence of the place sink in. I said to myself: "If I wait long enough, the guardian will turn up and show me the tombs—" and I rather hoped he wouldn't turn up too soon.

I sat down on a stone and lit a cigarette. As soon as I had done it, it struck me as a puerile and portentous thing to do, with that great blind house looking down at me, and all the empty avenues converging on me. It may have been the depth of the silence that made me so conscious of my gesture. The squeak of my match sounded as loud as the scraping of a brake, and I almost fancied I heard it fall when I tossed it onto the grass. But there was more than that: a sense of irrelevance, of littleness, of childish bravado, in sitting there puffing my cigarette-smoke into the face of such a past.

I knew nothing of the history of Kerfol—I was new to Brittany, and Lanrivain had never mentioned the name to me till the day before—but one couldn't as much as glance at that pile without feeling in it a long accumulation of history. What kind of history I was not prepared to guess: perhaps only the sheer weight of many associated lives and deaths which gives a kind of majesty to all old houses. But the aspect of Kerfol suggested something more—a perspective of stern and cruel memories stretching away, like its own grey avenues, into a blur of darkness.

Certainly no house had ever more completely and finally broken with the present. As it stood there, lifting its proud roofs and gables to the sky, it might have been its own funeral monument. "Tombs in the chapel? The whole place is a tomb!" I reflected. I hoped more and more that the guardian would not come. The details of the place, however striking, would seem trivial compared with its collective impressiveness; and I wanted only to sit there and be penetrated by the weight of its silence.

"It's the very place for you!" Lanrivain had said; and I was overcome by the almost blasphemous frivolity of suggesting to any living being that Kerfol was the place for him. "Is it possible that any one could NOT see—?" I wondered. I did not finish the thought: what I meant was undefinable. I stood up and wandered toward the gate. I was beginning to want to know more; not to SEE more—I was by now so sure it was not a question of seeing—but to feel more: feel all the place had to communicate. "But to get in one will have to rout out the keeper," I thought reluctantly, and hesitated. Finally I crossed the bridge and tried the iron gate. It yielded, and I walked under the tunnel formed by the thickness of the chemin de ronde. At the farther end, a wooden barricade had been laid across the entrance, and beyond it I saw a court enclosed in noble architecture. The main building faced me; and I now discovered that one half was a mere ruined front, with gaping windows through which the wild growths of the moat and the trees of the park were visible. The rest of the house was still in its robust beauty. One end abutted on the round tower, the other on the small traceried chapel, and in an angle of the building stood a graceful well-head adorned with mossy urns. A few roses grew against the walls, and on an upper window-sill I remember noticing a pot of fuchsias.

My sense of the pressure of the invisible began to yield to my architectural interest. The building was so fine that I felt a desire to explore it for its own sake. I looked about the court, wondering in which corner the guardian lodged. Then I pushed open the barrier and went in. As I did so, a little dog barred my way. He was such a remarkably beautiful little dog that for a moment he made me forget the splendid place he was defending. I was not sure of his breed at the time, but have since learned that it was Chinese, and that he was of a rare variety called the "Sleeve-dog." He was very small and golden brown, with large brown eyes and a ruffled throat: he looked rather like a large tawny chrysanthemum. I said to myself: "These little beasts always snap and scream, and somebody will be out in a minute."

The little animal stood before me, forbidding, almost menacing: there was anger in his large brown eyes. But he made no sound, he came no nearer. Instead, as I advanced, he gradually fell back, and I noticed that another dog, a vague rough brindled thing, had limped up. "There'll be a hubbub now," I thought; for at the same moment a third dog, a long-haired white mongrel, slipped out of a doorway and joined the others. All three stood looking at me with grave eyes; but not a sound came from them. As I advanced they continued to fall back on muffled paws, still watching me. "At a given point, they'll all charge at my ankles: it's one of the dodges that dogs who live together put up on one," I thought. I was not much alarmed, for they were neither large nor formidable. But they let me wander about the court as I pleased, following me at a little distance—always the same distance—and always keeping their eyes on me. Presently I looked across at the ruined facade, and saw that in one of its window-frames another dog stood: a large white pointer with one brown ear. He was an old grave dog, much more experienced than the others; and he seemed to be observing me with a deeper intentness.

"I'll hear from HIM," I said to myself; but he stood in the empty window-frame, against the trees of the park, and continued to watch me without moving. I looked back at him for a time, to see if the sense that he was being watched would not rouse him. Half the width of the court lay between us, and we stared at each other silently across it. But he did not stir, and at last I turned away. Behind me I found the rest of the pack, with a newcomer added: a small black greyhound with pale agate-coloured eyes. He was shivering a little, and his expression was more timid than that of the others. I noticed that he kept a little behind them. And still there was not a sound.

I stood there for fully five minutes, the circle about me—
waiting, as they seemed to be waiting. At last I went up to
the little golden-brown dog and stooped to pat him. As I
did so, I heard myself laugh. The little dog did not start, or
growl, or take his eyes from me—he simply slipped back
about a yard, and then paused and continued to look at me.
"Oh, hang it!" I exclaimed aloud, and walked across the
court toward the well.

As I advanced, the dogs separated and slid away into
different corners of the court. I examined the urns on the
well, tried a locked door or two, and up and down the dumb
facade; then I faced about toward the chapel. When I turned
I perceived that all the dogs had disappeared except the old
pointer, who still watched me from the empty window-frame.
It was rather a relief to be rid of that cloud of witnesses; and
I began to look about me for a way to the back of the house.
"Perhaps there'll be somebody in the garden," I thought.
I found a way across the moat, scrambled over a wall
smothered in brambles, and got into the garden. A few lean
hydrangeas and geraniums pined in the flower-beds, and the
ancient house looked down on them indifferently. Its garden
side was plainer and severer than the other: the long granite
front, with its few windows and steep roof, looked like a
fortress-prison. I walked around the farther wing, went up
some disjointed steps, and entered the deep twilight of a
narrow and incredibly old box-walk. The walk was just wide

13

enough for one person to slip through, and its branches met overhead. It was like the ghost of a box-walk, its lustrous green all turning to the shadowy greyness of the avenues. I walked on and on, the branches hitting me in the face and springing back with a dry rattle; and at length I came out on the grassy top of the chemin de ronde. I walked along it to the gate-tower, looking down into the court, which was just below me. Not a human being was in sight; and neither were the dogs. I found a flight of steps in the thickness of the wall and went down them; and when I emerged again into the court, there stood the circle of dogs, the golden-brown one a little ahead of the others, the black greyhound shivering in the rear.

"Oh, hang it—you uncomfortable beasts, you!" I exclaimed, my voice startling me with a sudden echo. The dogs stood motionless, watching me. I knew by this time that they would not try to prevent my approaching the house, and the knowledge left me free to examine them. I had a feeling that they must be horribly cowed to be so silent and inert. Yet they did not look hungry or ill-treated. Their coats were smooth and they were not thin, except the shivering greyhound. It was more as if they had lived a long time with people who never spoke to them or looked at them: as though the silence of the place had gradually benumbed their busy inquisitive natures. And this strange passivity, this almost human lassitude, seemed to me sadder than the misery of starved and beaten animals. I should have liked to rouse them for a minute, to coax them into a game or a scamper; but the longer I looked into their fixed and weary eyes the more preposterous the idea became. With the windows of that house looking down on us, how could I have imagined such a thing? The dogs knew better: THEY knew what the house would tolerate and what it would not. I even fancied that they knew what was passing through my mind, and pitied me for my frivolity. But even that feeling probably reached them through a thick fog of listlessness. I had an idea that their distance from me was as nothing to my remoteness from them. In the last analysis, the impression they produced was that of having in common one memory so deep and dark that nothing that had happened since was worth either a growl or a wag.

"I say," I broke out abruptly, addressing myself to the dumb circle, "do you know what you look like, the whole lot of you? You look as if you'd seen a ghost—that's how you look! I wonder if there IS a ghost here, and nobody but you left for it to appear to?" The dogs continued to gaze at me without moving...

It was dark when I saw Lanrivain's motor lamps at the cross-roads—and I wasn't exactly sorry to see them. I had the sense of having escaped from the loneliest place in the whole world, and of not liking loneliness—to that degree—as much as I had imagined I should. My friend had brought his solicitor back from Quimper for the night, and seated beside a fat and affable stranger I felt no inclination to talk of Kerfol...

But that evening, when Lanrivain and the solicitor were closeted in the study, Madame de Lanrivain began to question me in the drawing-room.

"Well—are you going to buy Kerfol?" she asked, tilting up her gay chin from her embroidery.

"I haven't decided yet. The fact is, I couldn't get into the house," I said, as if I had simply postponed my decision, and meant to go back for another look.

"You couldn't get in? Why, what happened? The family are mad to sell the place, and the old guardian has orders—"

"Very likely. But the old guardian wasn't there."

"What a pity! He must have gone to market. But his daughter—?"

"There was nobody about. At least I saw no one."

"How extraordinary! Literally nobody?"

"Nobody but a lot of dogs—a whole pack of them—who seemed to have the place to themselves."

Madame de Lanrivain let the embroidery slip to her knee and folded her hands on it. For several minutes she looked at me thoughtfully.

"A pack of dogs—you SAW them?"

"Saw them? I saw nothing else!"

"How many?" She dropped her voice a little. "I've always

wondered—"

I looked at her with surprise: I had supposed the place to be familiar to her. "Have you never been to Kerfol?" I asked.

"Oh, yes: often. But never on that day."

"What day?"

"I'd quite forgotten—and so had Herve, I'm sure. If we'd remembered, we never should have sent you today—but then, after all, one doesn't half believe that sort of thing, does one?"

"What sort of thing?" I asked, involuntarily sinking my voice to the level of hers. Inwardly I was thinking: "I KNEW there was something..."

Madame de Lanrivain cleared her throat and produced a reassuring smile. "Didn't Herve tell you the story of Kerfol? An ancestor of his was mixed up in it. You know every Breton house has its ghost-story; and some of them are rather unpleasant."

"Yes—but those dogs?" I insisted.

"Well, those dogs are the ghosts of Kerfol. At least, the peasants say there's one day in the year when a lot of dogs appear there; and that day the keeper and his daughter go off to Morlaix and get drunk. The women in Brittany drink dreadfully." She stooped to match a silk; then she lifted her charming inquisitive Parisian face: "Did you REALLY see a lot of dogs? There isn't one at Kerfol," she said.

CHAPTER II

Lanrivain, the next day, hunted out a shabby calf volume from the back of an upper shelf of his library.

"Yes—here it is. What does it call itself? A History of the Assizes of the Duchy of Brittany. Quimper, 1702. The book was written about a hundred years later than the Kerfol affair; but I believe the account is transcribed pretty literally from the judicial records. Anyhow, it's queer reading. And there's a Herve de Lanrivain mixed up in it—not exactly MY style, as you'll see. But then he's only a collateral. Here, take the book up to bed with you. I don't exactly remember the details; but after you've read it I'll bet anything you'll leave your light burning all night!"

I left my light burning all night, as he had predicted; but it was chiefly because, till near dawn, I was absorbed in my reading. The account of the trial of Anne de Cornault, wife of the lord of Kerfol, was long and closely printed. It was, as my friend had said, probably an almost literal transcription of what took place in the court-room; and the trial lasted nearly a month. Besides, the type of the book was detestable...

At first I thought of translating the old record literally. But it is full of wearisome repetitions, and the main lines of the story are forever straying off into side issues. So I have tried to disentangle it, and give it here in a simpler form. At times, however, I have reverted to the text because no other words could have conveyed so exactly the sense of what I felt at Kerfol; and nowhere have I added anything of my own.

CHAPTER III

It was in the year 16— that Yves de Cornault, lord of the domain of Kerfol, went to the pardon of Locronan to perform his religious duties. He was a rich and powerful noble, then in his sixty-second year, but hale and sturdy, a great horseman and hunter and a pious man. So all his neighbours attested. In appearance he seems to have been short and broad, with a swarthy face, legs slightly bowed from the saddle, a hanging nose and broad hands with black hairs on them. He had married young and lost his wife and son soon after, and since then had lived alone at Kerfol. Twice a year he went to Morlaix, where he had a handsome house by the river, and spent a week or ten days there; and occasionally he rode to Rennes on business. Witnesses were found to declare that during these absences he led a life different from the one he was known to lead at Kerfol, where he busied himself with his estate, attended mass daily, and found his only amusement in hunting the wild boar and water-fowl. But these rumours are not particularly relevant, and it is certain that among people of his own class in the neighbourhood he passed for a stern and even austere man, observant of his religious obligations, and keeping strictly to himself. There was no talk of any familiarity with the women on his estate, though at that time the nobility were very free with their peasants. Some people said he had never looked at a woman since his wife's death; but such things are hard to prove, and the evidence on this point was not worth much.

Well, in his sixty-second year, Yves de Cornault went to the pardon at Locronan, and saw there a young lady of Douarnenez, who had ridden over pillion behind her father to do her duty to the saint. Her name was Anne de Barrigan, and she came of good old Breton stock, but much less great and powerful than that of Yves de Cornault; and her father had squandered his fortune at cards, and lived almost like a peasant in his little granite manor on the moors... I have said I would add nothing of my own to this bald statement of a strange case; but I must interrupt myself here to describe the young lady who rode up to the lych-gate of Locronan at the very moment when the Baron de Cornault was also dismounting there. I take my description from a rather rare thing: a faded drawing in red crayon, sober and truthful enough to be by a late pupil of the Clouets, which hangs in Lanrivain's study, and is said to be a portrait of Anne de Barrigan. It is unsigned and has no mark of identity but the initials A. B., and the date 16—, the year after her marriage. It represents a young woman with a small oval face, almost pointed, yet wide enough for a full mouth with a tender depression at the corners. The nose is small, and the eyebrows are set rather high, far apart, and as lightly pencilled as the eyebrows in a Chinese painting. The forehead is high and serious, and the hair, which one feels to be fine and thick and fair, drawn off it and lying close like a cap. The eyes are neither large nor small, hazel probably, with a look at once shy and steady. A pair of beautiful long hands are crossed below the lady's breast...

The chaplain of Kerfol, and other witnesses, averred that when the Baron came back from Locronan he jumped from his horse, ordered another to be instantly saddled, called to a young page come with him, and rode away that same evening to the south. His steward followed the next morning with coffers laden on a pair of pack mules. The following week Yves de Cornault rode back to Kerfol, sent for his vassals and tenants, and told them he was to be married at All Saints to Anne de Barrigan of Douarnenez. And on All Saints' Day the marriage took place.

As to the next few years, the evidence on both sides seems to show that they passed happily for the couple. No one was found to say that Yves de Cornault had been unkind to his wife, and it was plain to all that he was content with his bargain. Indeed, it was admitted by the chaplain and other witnesses for the prosecution that the young lady had a softening influence on her husband, and that he became less exacting with his tenants, less harsh to peasants and dependents, and less subject to the fits of gloomy silence which had darkened his widow-hood. As to his wife, the only grievance her champions could call up in her behalf was that Kerfol was a lonely place, and that when her husband

was away on business at Rennes or Morlaix—whither she
was never taken—she was not allowed so much as to walk in
the park unaccompanied. But no one asserted that she was
unhappy, though one servant-woman said she had surprised
her crying, and had heard her say that she was a woman
accursed to have no child, and nothing in life to call her
own. But that was a natural enough feeling in a wife attached
to her husband; and certainly it must have been a great grief
to Yves de Cornault that she gave him no son. Yet he never
made her feel her childlessness as a reproach—she herself
admits this in her evidence—but seemed to try to make her
forget it by showering gifts and favours on her. Rich though
he was, he had never been open-handed; but nothing was
too fine for his wife, in the way of silks or gems or linen, or
whatever else she fancied. Every wandering merchant was
welcome at Kerfol, and when the master was called away
he never came back without bringing his wife a handsome
present—something curious and particular—from Morlaix
or Rennes or Quimper. One of the waiting-women gave, in
cross-examination, an interesting list of one year's gifts, which
I copy. From Morlaix, a carved ivory junk, with Chinamen
at the oars, that a strange sailor had brought back as a votive
offering for Notre Dame de la Clarte, above Ploumanac'h;
from Quimper, an embroidered gown, worked by the nuns
of the Assumption; from Rennes, a silver rose that opened
and showed an amber Virgin with a crown of garnets; from

Morlaix, again, a length of Damascus velvet shot with gold, bought of a Jew from Syria; and for Michaelmas that same year, from Rennes, a necklet or bracelet of round stones— emeralds and pearls and rubies—strung like beads on a gold wire. This was the present that pleased the lady best, the woman said. Later on, as it happened, it was produced at the trial, and appears to have struck the Judges and the public as a curious and valuable jewel.

The very same winter, the Baron absented himself again, this time as far as Bordeaux, and on his return he brought his wife something even odder and prettier than the bracelet. It was a winter evening when he rode up to Kerfol and, walking into the hall, found her sitting listlessly by the fire, her chin on her hand, looking into the fire. He carried a velvet box in his hand and, setting it down on the hearth, lifted the lid and let out a little golden-brown dog.

Anne de Cornault exclaimed with pleasure as the little creature bounded toward her. "Oh, it looks like a bird or a butterfly!" she cried as she picked it up; and the dog put its paws on her shoulders and looked at her with eyes "like a Christian's." After that she would never have it out of her sight, and petted and talked to it as if it had been a child—as indeed it was the nearest thing to a child she was to know. Yves de Cornault was much pleased with his purchase. The dog had been brought to him by a sailor from an East India merchantman, and the sailor had bought it of a pilgrim in a bazaar at Jaffa, who had stolen it from a nobleman's wife in China: a perfectly permissible thing to do, since the pilgrim was a Christian and the nobleman a heathen doomed to hellfire. Yves de Cornault had paid a long price for the dog, for they were beginning to be in demand at the French court, and the sailor knew he had got hold of a good thing; but Anne's pleasure was so great that, to see her laugh and play with the little animal, her husband would doubtless have given twice the sum.

So far, all the evidence is at one, and the narrative plain sailing; but now the steering becomes difficult. I will try to keep as nearly as possible to Anne's own statements; though toward the end, poor thing...

Well, to go back. The very year after the little brown dog was brought to Kerfol, Yves de Cornault, one winter night, was found dead at the head of a narrow flight of stairs leading down from his wife's rooms to a door opening on the court. It was his wife who found him and gave the alarm, so distracted, poor wretch, with fear and horror—for his blood was all over her—that at first the roused household could not make out what she was saying, and thought she had gone suddenly mad. But there, sure enough, at the top of the stairs lay her husband, stone dead, and head foremost, the blood from his wounds dripping down to the steps below him. He had been dreadfully scratched and gashed about the face and throat, as if with a dull weapon; and one of his legs had a deep tear in it which had cut an artery, and probably caused his death. But how did he come there, and who had murdered him?

His wife declared that she had been asleep in her bed, and hearing his cry had rushed out to find him lying on the stairs; but this was immediately questioned. In the first place, it was proved that from her room she could not have heard the struggle on the stairs, owing to the thickness of the walls and the length of the intervening passage; then it was evident that she had not been in bed and asleep, since she was dressed when she roused the house, and her bed had not been slept in. Moreover, the door at the bottom of the stairs was ajar, and the key in the lock; and it was noticed by the chaplain (an observant man) that the dress she wore was stained with blood about the knees, and that there were traces of small blood-stained hands low down on the staircase walls, so that it was conjectured that she had really been at the postern-door when her husband fell and, feeling her way up to him in the darkness on her hands and knees, had been stained by his blood dripping down on her. Of course it was argued on the other side that the blood-marks on her dress might have been caused by her kneeling down by her husband when she rushed out of her room; but there was the open door below, and the fact that the fingermarks in the staircase all pointed upward.

The accused held to her statement for the first two days,

in spite of its improbability; but on the third day word was brought to her that Herve de Lanrivain, a young nobleman of the neighbourhood, had been arrested for complicity in the crime. Two or three witnesses thereupon came forward to say that it was known throughout the country that Lanrivain had formerly been on good terms with the lady of Cornault; but that he had been absent from Brittany for over a year, and people had ceased to associate their names. The witnesses who made this statement were not of a very reputable sort. One was an old herb-gatherer suspected of witch-craft, another a drunken clerk from a neighbouring parish, the third a half-witted shepherd who could be made to say anything; and it was clear that the prosecution was not satisfied with its case, and would have liked to find more definite proof of Lanrivain's complicity than the statement of the herb-gatherer, who swore to having seen him climbing the wall of the park on the night of the murder. One way of patching out incomplete proofs in those days was to put some sort of pressure, moral or physical, on the accused person. It is not clear what pressure was put on Anne de Cornault; but on the third day, when she was brought into court, she "appeared weak and wandering," and after being encouraged to collect herself and speak the truth, on her honour and the wounds of her Blessed Redeemer, she confessed that she had in fact gone down the stairs to speak with Herve de Lanrivain (who denied everything), and had been surprised there by the sound of her husband's fall. That was better; and the prosecution rubbed its hands with satisfaction. The satisfaction increased when various dependents living at Kerfol were induced to say—with apparent sincerity—that during the year or two preceding his death their master had once more grown uncertain and irascible, and subject to the fits of brooding silence which his household had learned to dread before his second marriage. This seemed to show that things had not been going well at Kerfol; though no one could be found to say that there had been any signs of open disagreement between husband and wife.

Anne de Cornault, when questioned as to her reason for going down at night to open the door to Herve de Lanrivain, made an answer which must have sent a smile around the court. She said it was because she was lonely and wanted to talk with the young man. Was this the only reason? she was asked; and replied: "Yes, by the Cross over your Lordships' heads." "But why at midnight?" the court asked. "Because I could see him in no other way." I can see the exchange of glances across the ermine collars under the Crucifix.

Anne de Cornault, further questioned, said that her married life had been extremely lonely: "desolate" was the word she used. It was true that her husband seldom spoke harshly to her; but there were days when he did not speak at all. It was true that he had never struck or threatened her; but he kept her like a prisoner at Kerfol, and when he rode away to Morlaix or Quimper or Rennes he set so close a watch on her that she could not pick a flower in the garden without having a waiting-woman at her heels. "I am no Queen, to need such honours," she once said to him; and he had answered that a man who has a treasure does not leave the key in the lock when he goes out. "Then take me with you," she urged; but to this he said that towns were pernicious places, and young wives better off at their own firesides.

"But what did you want to say to Herve de Lanrivain?" the court asked; and she answered: "To ask him to take me away."

"Ah—you confess that you went down to him with adulterous thoughts?"

"No."

"Then why did you want him to take you away?"

"Because I was afraid for my life."

"Of whom were you afraid?"

"Of my husband."

"Why were you afraid of your husband?"

"Because he had strangled my little dog."

Another smile must have passed around the court-room: in days when any nobleman had a right to hang his peasants— and most of them exercised it—pinching a pet animal's wind-pipe was nothing to make a fuss about.

At this point one of the Judges, who appears to have

had a certain sympathy for the accused, suggested that she should be allowed to explain herself in her own way; and she thereupon made the following statement.

The first years of her marriage had been lonely; but her husband had not been unkind to her. If she had had a child she would not have been unhappy; but the days were long, and it rained too much.

It was true that her husband, whenever he went away and left her, brought her a handsome present on his return; but this did not make up for the loneliness. At least nothing had, till he brought her the little brown dog from the East: after that she was much less unhappy. Her husband seemed pleased that she was so fond of the dog; he gave her leave to put her jewelled bracelet around its neck, and to keep it always with her.

One day she had fallen asleep in her room, with the dog at her feet, as his habit was. Her feet were bare and resting on his back. Suddenly she was waked by her husband: he stood beside her, smiling not unkindly.

"You look like my great-grandmother, Juliane de Cornault, lying in the chapel with her feet on a little dog," he said.

The analogy sent a chill through her, but she laughed and answered: "Well, when I am dead you must put me beside her, carved in marble, with my dog at my feet."

"Oho—we'll wait and see," he said, laughing also, but with his black brows close together. "The dog is the emblem of fidelity."

"And do you doubt my right to lie with mine at my feet?"

"When I'm in doubt I find out," he answered. "I am an old man," he added, "and people say I make you lead a lonely life. But I swear you shall have your monument if you earn it."

"And I swear to be faithful," she returned, "if only for the sake of having my little dog at my feet."

Not long afterward he went on business to the Quimper Assizes; and while he was away his aunt, the widow of a great nobleman of the duchy, came to spend a night at Kerfol on her way to the pardon of Ste. Barbe. She was a woman of great piety and consequence, and much respected by Yves de Cornault, and when she proposed to Anne to go with her to Ste. Barbe no one could object, and even the chaplain declared himself in favour of the pilgrimage. So Anne set out for Ste. Barbe, and there for the first time she talked with Herve de Lanrivain. He had come once or twice to Kerfol with his father, but she had never before exchanged a dozen words with him. They did not talk for more than five minutes now: it was under the chestnuts, as the procession was coming out of the chapel. He said: "I pity you," and she was surprised, for she had not supposed that any one thought her an object of pity. He added: "Call for me when you need me," and she smiled a little, but was glad afterward, and thought often of the meeting.

31

She confessed to having seen him three times afterward: not more. How or where she would not say—one had the impression that she feared to implicate some one. Their meetings had been rare and brief; and at the last he had told her that he was starting the next day for a foreign country, on a mission which was not without peril and might keep him for many months absent. He asked her for a remembrance, and she had none to give him but the collar about the little dog's neck. She was sorry afterward that she had given it, but he was so unhappy at going that she had not had the courage to refuse.

Her husband was away at the time. When he returned a few days later he picked up the little dog to pet it, and noticed that its collar was missing. His wife told him that the dog had lost it in the undergrowth of the park, and that she and her maids had hunted a whole day for it. It was true, she explained to the court, that she had made the maids search for the necklet—they all believed the dog had lost it in the park...

Her husband made no comment, and that evening at supper he was in his usual mood, between good and bad: you could never tell which. He talked a good deal, describing what he had seen and done at Rennes; but now and then he stopped and looked hard at her; and when she went to bed she found her little dog strangled on her pillow. The little thing was dead, but still warm; she stooped to lift it, and her distress turned to horror when she discovered that it had been strangled by twisting twice round its throat the necklet she had given to Lanrivain.

The next morning at dawn she buried the dog in the garden, and hid the necklet in her breast. She said nothing to her husband, then or later, and he said nothing to her; but that day he had a peasant hanged for stealing a faggot in the park, and the next day he nearly beat to death a young horse he was breaking.

Winter set in, and the short days passed, and the long nights, one by one; and she heard nothing of Herve de Lanrivain. It might be that her husband had killed him; or merely that he had been robbed of the necklet. Day after day by the hearth among the spinning maids, night after night alone on her bed, she wondered and trembled. Sometimes at table her husband looked across at her and smiled; and then she felt sure that Lanrivain was dead. She dared not try to get news of him, for she was sure her husband would find out if she did: she had an idea that he could find out anything. Even when a witch-woman who was a noted seer, and could show you the whole world in her crystal, came to the castle for a night's shelter, and the maids flocked to her, Anne held back. The winter was long and black and rainy. One day, in Yves de Cornault's absence, some gypsies came to Kerfol with a troop of performing dogs. Anne bought the smallest and cleverest, a white dog with a feathery coat and one blue and one brown eye. It seemed to have been ill-treated by the gypsies, and clung to her plaintively when she took it from them. That evening her husband came back, and when she went to bed she found the dog strangled on her pillow.

After that she said to herself that she would never have another dog; but one bitter cold evening a poor lean greyhound was found whining at the castle-gate, and she took him in and forbade the maids to speak of him to her husband. She hid him in a room that no one went to, smuggled food to him from her own plate, made him a warm bed to lie on and petted him like a child.

Yves de Cornault came home, and the next day she found the greyhound strangled on her pillow. She wept in secret, but said nothing, and resolved that even if she met a dog dying of hunger she would never bring him into the castle; but one day she found a young sheep-dog, a brindled puppy with good blue eyes, lying with a broken leg in the snow of the park. Yves de Cornault was at Rennes, and she brought the dog in, warmed and fed it, tied up its leg and hid it in the castle till her husband's return. The day before, she gave it to a peasant woman who lived a long way off, and paid her handsomely to care for it and say nothing; but that night she heard a whining and scratching at her door, and when she opened it the lame puppy, drenched and shivering, jumped up on her with little sobbing barks. She hid him in her bed, and the next morning was about to have him taken back to the peasant woman when she heard her husband ride into the court. She shut the dog in a chest and went down to receive him. An hour or two later, when she returned to her room, the puppy lay strangled on her pillow...

After that she dared not make a pet of any other dog; and her loneliness became almost unendurable. Sometimes, when she crossed the court of the castle, and thought no one was looking, she stopped to pat the old pointer at the gate. But one day as she was caressing him her husband came out of the chapel; and the next day the old dog was gone...

This curious narrative was not told in one sitting of the court, or received without impatience and incredulous comment. It was plain that the Judges were surprised by its puerility, and that it did not help the accused in the eyes of the public. It was an odd tale, certainly; but what did it prove? That Yves de Cornault disliked dogs, and that his wife, to gratify her own fancy, persistently ignored this dislike. As for pleading this trivial disagreement as an excuse for her relations—whatever their nature—with her supposed accomplice, the argument was so absurd that her own lawyer manifestly regretted having let her make use of it, and tried several times to cut short her story. But she went on to the end, with a kind of hypnotized insistence, as though the scenes she evoked were so real to her that she had forgotten where she was and imagined herself to be re-living them.

At length the Judge who had previously shown a certain

kindness to her said (leaning forward a little, one may suppose, from his row of dozing colleagues): "Then you would have us believe that you murdered your husband because he would not let you keep a pet dog?"

"I did not murder my husband."

"Who did, then? Herve de Lanrivain?"

"No."

"Who then? Can you tell us?"

"Yes, I can tell you. The dogs—" At that point she was carried out of the court in a swoon.

．．．．．．．

It was evident that her lawyer tried to get her to abandon this line of defense. Possibly her explanation, whatever it was, had seemed convincing when she poured it out to him in the heat of their first private colloquy; but now that it was exposed to the cold daylight of judicial scrutiny, and the banter of the town, he was thoroughly ashamed of it, and would have sacrificed her without a scruple to save his professional reputation. But the obstinate Judge—who perhaps, after all, was more inquisitive than kindly—evidently wanted to hear the story out, and she was ordered, the next day, to continue her deposition.

She said that after the disappearance of the old watchdog nothing particular happened for a month or two. Her husband was much as usual: she did not remember any special incident. But one evening a pedlar woman came to

the castle and was selling trinkets to the maids. She had no
heart for trinkets, but she stood looking on while the women
made their choice. And then, she did not know how, but the
pedlar coaxed her into buying for herself an odd pear-shaped
pomander with a strong scent in it—she had once seen
something of the kind on a gypsy woman. She had no desire
for the pomander, and did not know why she had bought it.
The pedlar said that whoever wore it had the power to read
the future; but she did not really believe that, or care much
either. However, she bought the thing and took it up to her
room, where she sat turning it about in her hand. Then the
strange scent attracted her and she began to wonder what
kind of spice was in the box. She opened it and found a grey
bean rolled in a strip of paper; and on the paper she saw
a sign she knew, and a message from Herve de Lanrivain,
saying that he was at home again and would be at the door
in the court that night after the moon had set...

She burned the paper and then sat down to think. It was
nightfall, and her husband was at home... She had no way
of warning Lanrivain, and there was nothing to do but to
wait...

At this point I fancy the drowsy courtroom beginning to
wake up. Even to the oldest hand on the bench there must
have been a certain aesthetic relish in picturing the feelings
of a woman on receiving such a message at night-fall from a
man living twenty miles away, to whom she had no means

of sending a warning...

She was not a clever woman, I imagine; and as the first result of her cogitation she appears to have made the mistake of being, that evening, too kind to her husband. She could not ply him with wine, according to the traditional expedient, for though he drank heavily at times he had a strong head; and when he drank beyond its strength it was because he chose to, and not because a woman coaxed him. Not his wife, at any rate—she was an old story by now. As I read the case, I fancy there was no feeling for her left in him but the hatred occasioned by his supposed dishonour.

At any rate, she tried to call up her old graces; but early in the evening he complained of pains and fever, and left the hall to go up to his room. His servant carried him a cup of hot wine, and brought back word that he was sleeping and not to be disturbed; and an hour later, when Anne lifted the tapestry and listened at his door, she heard his loud regular breathing. She thought it might be a feint, and stayed a long time barefooted in the cold passage, her ear to the crack; but the breathing went on too steadily and naturally to be other than that of a man in a sound sleep. She crept back to her room reassured, and stood in the window watching the moon set through the trees of the park. The sky was misty and starless, and after the moon went down the night was pitch black. She knew the time had come, and stole along the passage, past her husband's door—where she stopped again to listen to his breathing—to the top of the stairs. There she paused a moment, and assured herself that no one was following her; then she began to go down the stairs in the darkness. They were so steep and winding that she had to go very slowly, for fear of stumbling. Her one thought was to get the door unbolted, tell Lanrivain to make his escape, and hasten back to her room. She had tried the bolt earlier in the evening, and managed to put a little grease on it; but nevertheless, when she drew it, it gave a squeak... not loud, but it made her heart stop; and the next minute, overhead, she heard a noise...

"What noise?" the prosecution interposed.

"My husband's voice calling out my name and cursing me."

"What did you hear after that?"

"A terrible scream and a fall."

"Where was Herve de Lanrivain at this time?"

"He was standing outside in the court. I just made him out in the darkness. I told him for God's sake to go, and then I pushed the door shut."

"What did you do next?"

"I stood at the foot of the stairs and listened."

"What did you hear?"

"I heard dogs snarling and panting." (Visible discouragement of the bench, boredom of the public, and exasperation of the lawyer for the defense. Dogs again—! But the inquisitive

Judge insisted.)

"What dogs?"

She bent her head and spoke so low that she had to be told to repeat her answer: "I don't know."

"How do you mean—you don't know?"

"I don't know what dogs..."

The Judge again intervened: "Try to tell us exactly what happened. How long did you remain at the foot of the stairs?"

"Only a few minutes."

"And what was going on meanwhile overhead?"

"The dogs kept on snarling and panting. Once or twice he cried out. I think he moaned once. Then he was quiet."

"Then what happened?"

"Then I heard a sound like the noise of a pack when the wolf is thrown to them—gulping and lapping."

(There was a groan of disgust and repulsion through the court, and another attempted intervention by the distracted lawyer. But the inquisitive Judge was still inquisitive.)

"And all the while you did not go up?"

"Yes—I went up then—to drive them off."

"The dogs?"

"Yes."

"Well—?"

"When I got there it was quite dark. I found my husband's flint and steel and struck a spark. I saw him lying there. He was dead."

"And the dogs?"

"The dogs were gone."

"Gone—where to?"

"I don't know. There was no way out—and there were no dogs at Kerfol."

She straightened herself to her full height, threw her arms above her head, and fell down on the stone floor with a long scream. There was a moment of confusion in the court-room. Some one on the bench was heard to say: "This is clearly a case for the ecclesiastical authorities"—and the prisoner's lawyer doubtless jumped at the suggestion.

After this, the trial loses itself in a maze of cross-questioning and squabbling. Every witness who was called corroborated Anne de Cornault's statement that there were no dogs at Kerfol: had been none for several months. The master of the house had taken a dislike to dogs, there was no denying it. But, on the other hand, at the inquest, there had been long and bitter discussion as to the nature of the dead man's wounds. One of the surgeons called in had spoken of marks that looked like bites. The suggestion of witchcraft was revived, and the opposing lawyers hurled tomes of necromancy at each other.

At last Anne de Cornault was brought back into court—at the instance of the same Judge—and asked if she knew where the dogs she spoke of could have come from. On the body of her Redeemer she swore that she did not. Then the Judge put his final question: "If the dogs you think you heard had been known to you, do you think you would have recognized them by their barking?"

"Yes."

"Did you recognize them?"

"Yes."

"What dogs do you take them to have been?"

"My dead dogs," she said in a whisper... She was taken out of court, not to reappear there again. There was some kind of ecclesiastical investigation, and the end of the business was that the Judges disagreed with each other, and with the ecclesiastical committee, and that Anne de Cornault was finally handed over to the keeping of her husband's family, who shut her up in the keep of Kerfol, where she is said to have died many years later, a harmless madwoman.

So ends her story. As for that of Herve de Lanrivain, I had only to apply to his collateral descendant for its subsequent details. The evidence against the young man being insufficient, and his family influence in the duchy considerable, he was set free, and left soon afterward for Paris. He was probably in no mood for a worldly life, and he appears to have come almost immediately under the influence of the famous M. Arnauld d'Andilly and the gentlemen of Port Royal. A year or two later he was received into their Order, and without achieving any particular distinction he followed its good and evil fortunes till his death some twenty years later. Lanrivain showed me a portrait of him by a pupil of Philippe de Champaigne: sad eyes, an impulsive mouth and a narrow brow. Poor Herve de Lanrivain: it was a grey ending. Yet as I looked at his stiff and sallow effigy, in the dark dress of the Jansenists, I almost found myself envying his fate. After all, in the course of his life two great things had happened to him: he had loved romantically, and he must have talked with Pascal...

THE END

MRS. MANSTEY'S VIEW

As first published in Scribner's Magazine, July 1891

The view from Mrs. Manstey's window was not a striking one, but to her at least it was full of interest and beauty. Mrs. Manstey occupied the back room on the third floor of a New York boarding-house, in a street where the ash-barrels lingered late on the sidewalk and the gaps in the pavement would have staggered a Quintus Curtius. She was the widow of a clerk in a large wholesale house, and his death had left her alone, for her only daughter had married in California, and could not afford the long journey to New York to see her mother. Mrs. Manstey, perhaps, might have joined her daughter in the West, but they had now been so many years apart that they had ceased to feel any need of each other's society, and their intercourse had long been limited to the exchange of a few perfunctory letters, written with indifference by the daughter, and with difficulty by Mrs. Manstey, whose right hand was growing stiff with gout. Even had she felt a stronger desire for her daughter's companionship, Mrs. Manstey's increasing infirmity, which caused her to dread the three flights of stairs between her room and the street, would have given her pause on the eve of undertaking so long a journey; and without perhaps, formulating these reasons she had long since accepted as a matter of course her solitary life in New York.

She was, indeed, not quite lonely, for a few friends still toiled up now and then to her room; but their visits grew rare as the years went by. Mrs. Manstey had never been a sociable woman, and during her husband's lifetime his companionship had been all-sufficient to her. For many years she had cherished a desire to live in the country, to have a hen-house and a garden; but this longing had faded with age, leaving only in the breast of the uncommunicative old woman a vague tenderness for plants and animals. It was, perhaps, this tenderness which made her cling so fervently to her view from her window, a view in which the most optimistic eye would at first have failed to discover anything admirable.

Mrs. Manstey, from her coign of vantage (a slightly projecting bow-window where she nursed an ivy and a succession of unwholesome-looking bulbs), looked out first upon the yard of her own dwelling, of which, however, she could get but a restricted glimpse. Still, her gaze took in the topmost boughs of the ailanthus below her window, and she knew how early each year the clump of dicentra strung its bending stalk with hearts of pink.

But of greater interest were the yards beyond. Being for the most part attached to boarding-houses they were in a state of chronic untidiness and fluttering, on certain days of the week, with miscellaneous garments and frayed table-cloths. In spite of this Mrs. Manstey found much to admire in the long vista which she commanded. Some of the yards were, indeed, but stony wastes, with grass in the cracks of the pavement and no shade in spring save that afforded by the intermittent leafage of the clothes-lines. These yards Mrs. Manstey disapproved of, but the others, the green ones, she loved. She had grown used to their disorder; the broken barrels, the empty bottles and paths unswept no longer annoyed her; hers was the happy faculty of dwelling on the pleasanter side of the prospect before her.

In the very next enclosure did not a magnolia open its hard white flowers against the watery blue of April? And was there not, a little way down the line, a fence foamed over every May be lilac waves of wistaria? Farther still, a horse-chestnut lifted its candelabra of buff and pink blossoms above broad fans of foliage; while in the opposite yard June was sweet with the breath of a neglected syringa, which persisted in growing in spite of the countless obstacles opposed to its welfare.

But if nature occupied the front rank in Mrs. Manstey's view, there was much of a more personal character to interest her in the aspect of the houses and their inmates. She deeply disapproved of the mustard-colored curtains which had lately been hung in the doctor's window opposite; but she glowed with pleasure when the house farther down had its old bricks washed with a coat of paint. The occupants of the houses did not often show themselves at the back windows, but the servants were always in sight. Noisy slatterns, Mrs. Manstey pronounced the greater number; she knew their ways and hated them. But to the quiet cook in the newly painted house, whose mistress bullied her, and who secretly fed the stray cats at nightfall, Mrs. Manstey's warmest sympathies were given. On one occasion her feelings were racked by the neglect of a housemaid, who for two days forgot to feed the parrot committed to her care. On the third day, Mrs. Manstey, in spite of her gouty hand, had just penned a letter, beginning: "Madam, it is now three days since your parrot has been fed," when the forgetful maid appeared at the window with a cup of seed in her hand.

But in Mrs. Manstey's more meditative moods it was the narrowing perspective of far-off yards which pleased her best. She loved, at twilight, when the distant brown-stone spire seemed melting in the fluid yellow of the west, to lose herself in vague memories of a trip to Europe, made years ago, and now reduced in her mind's eye to a pale phantasmagoria of indistinct steeples and dreamy skies. Perhaps at heart Mrs. Manstey was an artist; at all events she was sensible of many changes of color unnoticed by the average eye, and dear to her as the green of early spring was the black lattice of branches against a cold sulphur sky at the close of a snowy day. She enjoyed, also, the sunny thaws of March, when patches of earth showed through the snow, like ink-spots spreading on a sheet of white blotting-paper; and, better still, the haze of boughs, leafless but swollen, which replaced the clear-cut tracery of winter. She even watched with a certain interest the trail of smoke from a far-off factory chimney, and missed a detail in the landscape when the factory was closed and the smoke disappeared.

Mrs. Manstey, in the long hours which she spent at her window, was not idle. She read a little, and knitted numberless stockings; but the view surrounded and shaped her life as the sea does a lonely island. When her rare callers came it was difficult for her to detach herself from the contemplation of the opposite window-washing, or the scrutiny of certain green points in a neighboring flower-bed which might, or might not, turn into hyacinths, while she feigned an interest in her visitor's anecdotes about some unknown grandchild. Mrs. Manstey's real friends were the denizens of the yards, the hyacinths, the magnolia, the green parrot, the maid who fed the cats, the doctor who studied late behind his mustard-colored curtains; and the confidant of her tenderer musings was the church-spire floating in the sunset.

One April day, as she sat in her usual place, with knitting cast aside and eyes fixed on the blue sky mottled with round clouds, a knock at the door announced the entrance of her landlady. Mrs. Manstey did not care for her landlady, but she submitted to her visits with ladylike resignation. Today, however, it seemed harder than usual to turn from the blue sky and the blossoming magnolia to Mrs. Sampson's unsuggestive face, and Mrs. Manstey was conscious of a distinct effort as she did so.

"The magnolia is out earlier than usual this year, Mrs. Sampson," she remarked, yielding to a rare impulse, for she seldom alluded to the absorbing interest of her life. In the first place it was a topic not likely to appeal to her visitors and, besides, she lacked the power of expression and could not have given utterance to her feelings had she wished to.

"The what, Mrs. Manstey?" inquired the landlady, glancing about the room as if to find there the explanation of Mrs. Manstey's statement.

"The magnolia in the next yard—in Mrs. Black's yard," Mrs. Manstey repeated.

"Is it, indeed? I didn't know there was a magnolia there," said Mrs. Sampson, carelessly. Mrs. Manstey looked at her; she did not know that there was a magnolia in the next yard!

"By the way," Mrs. Sampson continued, "speaking of Mrs. Black reminds me that the work on the extension is to begin next week."

"The what?" it was Mrs. Manstey's turn to ask.

"The extension," said Mrs. Sampson, nodding her head in the direction of the ignored magnolia. "You knew, of course, that Mrs. Black was going to build an extension to her house? Yes, ma'am. I hear it is to run right back to the end of the yard. How she can afford to build an extension in these hard times I don't see; but she always was crazy about building. She used to keep a boarding-house in Seventeenth Street, and she nearly ruined herself then by sticking out bow-windows and what not; I should have thought that would have cured her of building, but I guess it's a disease, like drink. Anyhow, the work is to begin on Monday."

Mrs. Manstey had grown pale. She always spoke slowly, so the landlady did not heed the long pause which followed. At last Mrs. Manstey said: "Do you know how high the extension will be?"

"That's the most absurd part of it. The extension is to be built right up to the roof of the main building; now, did you ever?"

Mrs. Manstey paused again. "Won't it be a great annoyance to you, Mrs. Sampson?" she asked.

"I should say it would. But there's no help for it; if people have got a mind to build extensions there's no law to prevent 'em, that I'm aware of." Mrs. Manstey, knowing this, was silent. "There is no help for it," Mrs. Sampson repeated, "but if I AM a church member, I wouldn't be so sorry if it ruined Eliza Black. Well, good-day, Mrs. Manstey; I'm glad to find you so comfortable."

So comfortable—so comfortable! Left to herself the old woman turned once more to the window. How lovely the view was that day! The blue sky with its round clouds shed a brightness over everything; the ailanthus had put on a tinge of yellow-green, the hyacinths were budding, the magnolia flowers looked more than ever like rosettes carved in alabaster. Soon the wistaria would bloom, then the horse-chestnut; but not for her. Between her eyes and them a barrier of brick and mortar would swiftly rise; presently even the spire would disappear, and all her radiant world be blotted out. Mrs. Manstey sent away untouched the dinner-tray brought to her that evening. She lingered in the window until the windy sunset died in bat-colored dusk; then, going to bed, she lay sleepless all night.

Early the next day she was up and at the window. It was raining, but even through the slanting gray gauze the scene had its charm—and then the rain was so good for the trees. She had noticed the day before that the ailanthus was growing dusty.

"Of course I might move," said Mrs. Manstey aloud, and turning from the window she looked about her room. She might move, of course; so might she be flayed alive; but she was not likely to survive either operation. The room, though far less important to her happiness than the view, was as much a part of her existence. She had lived in it seventeen years. She knew every stain on the wall-paper, every rent in the carpet; the light fell in a certain way on her engravings, her books had grown shabby on their shelves, her bulbs and ivy were used to their window and knew which way to lean to the sun. "We are all too old to move," she said.

That afternoon it cleared. Wet and radiant the blue reappeared through torn rags of cloud; the ailanthus sparkled; the earth in the flower-borders looked rich and warm. It was Thursday, and on Monday the building of the extension was to begin.

On Sunday afternoon a card was brought to Mrs. Black, as she was engaged in gathering up the fragments of the boarders' dinner in the basement. The card, black-edged, bore Mrs. Manstey's name.

"One of Mrs. Sampson's boarders; wants to move, I suppose. Well, I can give her a room next year in the extension. Dinah," said Mrs. Black, "tell the lady I'll be upstairs in a minute."

Mrs. Black found Mrs. Manstey standing in the long parlor garnished with statuettes and antimacassars; in that house she could not sit down.

Stooping hurriedly to open the register, which let out a cloud of dust, Mrs. Black advanced on her visitor.

"I'm happy to meet you, Mrs. Manstey; take a seat, please," the landlady remarked in her prosperous voice, the voice of a woman who can afford to build extensions. There was no help for it; Mrs. Manstey sat down.

"Is there anything I can do for you, ma'am?" Mrs. Black continued. "My house is full at present, but I am going to build an extension, and—"

"It is about the extension that I wish to speak," said Mrs. Manstey, suddenly. "I am a poor woman, Mrs. Black, and I have never been a happy one. I shall have to talk about myself first to—to make you understand."

Mrs. Black, astonished but imperturbable, bowed at this parenthesis.

"I never had what I wanted," Mrs. Manstey continued. "It was always one disappointment after another. For years I wanted to live in the country. I dreamed and dreamed about it; but we never could manage it. There was no sunny window in our house, and so all my plants died. My daughter married years ago and went away—besides, she never cared for the same things. Then my husband died and I was left alone. That was seventeen years ago. I went to live at Mrs. Sampson's, and I have been there ever since. I have grown a little infirm, as you see, and I don't get out often; only on fine days, if I am feeling very well. So you can understand my sitting a great deal in my window—the back window on the third floor—"

"Well, Mrs. Manstey," said Mrs. Black, liberally, "I could give you a back room, I dare say; one of the new rooms in the ex—"

"But I don't want to move; I can't move," said Mrs. Manstey, almost with a scream. "And I came to tell you that if you build that extension I shall have no view from my window—no view! Do you understand?"

Mrs. Black thought herself face to face with a lunatic, and she had always heard that lunatics must be humored.

"Dear me, dear me," she remarked, pushing her chair back a little way, "that is too bad, isn't it? Why, I never thought of that. To be sure, the extension WILL interfere with your view, Mrs. Manstey."

"You do understand?" Mrs. Manstey gasped.

"Of course I do. And I'm real sorry about it, too. But there, don't you worry, Mrs. Manstey. I guess we can fix that all right."

Mrs. Manstey rose from her seat, and Mrs. Black slipped toward the door.

"What do you mean by fixing it? Do you mean that I can induce you to change your mind about the extension? Oh, Mrs. Black, listen to me. I have two thousand dollars in the bank and I could manage, I know I could manage, to give you a thousand if—" Mrs. Manstey paused; the tears were rolling down her cheeks.

"There, there, Mrs. Manstey, don't you worry," repeated Mrs. Black, soothingly. "I am sure we can settle it. I am sorry that I can't stay and talk about it any longer, but this is such a busy time of day, with supper to get—"

Her hand was on the door-knob, but with sudden vigor Mrs. Manstey seized her wrist.

"You are not giving me a definite answer. Do you mean to

say that you accept my proposition?"

"Why, I'll think it over, Mrs. Manstey, certainly I will. I wouldn't annoy you for the world—"

"But the work is to begin to-morrow, I am told," Mrs. Manstey persisted.

Mrs. Black hesitated. "It shan't begin, I promise you that; I'll send word to the builder this very night." Mrs. Manstey tightened her hold.

"You are not deceiving me, are you?" she said.

"No—no," stammered Mrs. Black. "How can you think such a thing of me, Mrs. Manstey?"

Slowly Mrs. Manstey's clutch relaxed, and she passed through the open door. "One thousand dollars," she repeated, pausing in the hall; then she let herself out of the house and hobbled down the steps, supporting herself on the cast-iron railing.

"My goodness," exclaimed Mrs. Black, shutting and bolting the hall-door, "I never knew the old woman was crazy! And she looks so quiet and ladylike, too."

Mrs. Manstey slept well that night, but early the next morning she was awakened by a sound of hammering. She got to her window with what haste she might and, looking out saw that Mrs. Black's yard was full of workmen. Some were carrying loads of brick from the kitchen to the yard, others beginning to demolish the old-fashioned wooden balcony which adorned each story of Mrs. Black's house.

Mrs. Manstey saw that she had been deceived. At first she thought of confiding her trouble to Mrs. Sampson, but a settled discouragement soon took possession of her and she went back to bed, not caring to see what was going on.

Toward afternoon, however, feeling that she must know the worst, she rose and dressed herself. It was a laborious task, for her hands were stiffer than usual, and the hooks and buttons seemed to evade her.

When she seated herself in the window, she saw that the workmen had removed the upper part of the balcony, and that the bricks had multiplied since morning. One of the men, a coarse fellow with a bloated face, picked a magnolia blossom and, after smelling it, threw it to the ground; the next man, carrying a load of bricks, trod on the flower in passing.

"Look out, Jim," called one of the men to another who was smoking a pipe, "if you throw matches around near those barrels of paper you'll have the old tinder-box burning down before you know it." And Mrs. Manstey, leaning forward, perceived that there were several barrels of paper and rubbish under the wooden balcony.

At length the work ceased and twilight fell. The sunset was perfect and a roseate light, transfiguring the distant spire, lingered late in the west. When it grew dark Mrs. Manstey drew down the shades and proceeded, in her usual methodical manner, to light her lamp. She always filled and lit it with her own hands, keeping a kettle of kerosene on a zinc-covered shelf in a closet. As the lamp-light filled the room it assumed its usual peaceful aspect. The books and pictures and plants seemed, like their mistress, to settle themselves down for another quiet evening, and Mrs. Manstey, as was her wont, drew up her armchair to the table and began to knit.

That night she could not sleep. The weather had changed and a wild wind was abroad, blotting the stars with close-driven clouds. Mrs. Manstey rose once or twice and looked out of the window; but of the view nothing was discernible save a tardy light or two in the opposite windows. These lights at last went out, and Mrs. Manstey, who had watched for their extinction, began to dress herself. She was in evident haste, for she merely flung a thin dressing-gown over her night-dress and wrapped her head in a scarf; then she opened her closet and cautiously took out the kettle of kerosene. Having slipped a bundle of wooden matches into her pocket she proceeded, with increasing precautions, to unlock her door, and a few moments later she was feeling her way down the dark staircase, led by a glimmer of gas from the lower hall. At length she reached the bottom of the stairs and began the more difficult descent into the utter darkness of the basement. Here, however, she could move more freely, as there was less danger of being overheard; and without much delay she contrived to unlock the iron door leading into the yard. A gust of cold wind smote her as she stepped out and groped shiveringly under the clothes-lines.

That morning at three o'clock an alarm of fire brought the engines to Mrs. Black's door, and also brought Mrs. Sampson's startled boarders to their windows. The wooden balcony at the back of Mrs. Black's house was ablaze, and among those who watched the progress of the flames was Mrs. Manstey, leaning in her thin dressing-gown from the open window.

The fire, however, was soon put out, and the frightened occupants of the house, who had fled in scant attire, reassembled at dawn to find that little mischief had been done beyond the cracking of window panes and smoking of ceilings. In fact, the chief sufferer by the fire was Mrs. Manstey, who was found in the morning gasping with pneumonia, a not unnatural result, as everyone remarked, of her having hung out of an open window at her age in a dressing-gown. It was easy to see that she was very ill, but no one had guessed how grave the doctor's verdict would be, and the faces gathered that evening about Mrs. Sampson's table were awestruck and disturbed. Not that any of the boarders knew Mrs. Manstey well; she "kept to herself," as they said, and seemed to fancy herself too good for them; but then it is always disagreeable to have anyone dying in the house and, as one lady observed to another: "It might just as well have been you or me, my dear."

But it was only Mrs. Manstey; and she was dying, as she

had lived, lonely if not alone. The doctor had sent a trained nurse, and Mrs. Sampson, with muffled step, came in from time to time; but both, to Mrs. Manstey, seemed remote and unsubstantial as the figures in a dream. All day she said nothing; but when she was asked for her daughter's address she shook her head. At times the nurse noticed that she seemed to be listening attentively for some sound which did not come; then again she dozed.

The next morning at daylight she was very low. The nurse called Mrs. Sampson and as the two bent over the old woman they saw her lips move.

"Lift me up—out of bed," she whispered.

They raised her in their arms, and with her stiff hand she pointed to the window.

"Oh, the window—she wants to sit in the window. She used to sit there all day," Mrs. Sampson explained. "It can do her no harm, I suppose?"

"Nothing matters now," said the nurse.

They carried Mrs. Manstey to the window and placed her in her chair. The dawn was abroad, a jubilant spring dawn; the spire had already caught a golden ray, though the magnolia and horse-chestnut still slumbered in shadow. In Mrs. Black's yard all was quiet. The charred timbers of the balcony lay where they had fallen. It was evident that since the fire the builders had not returned to their work. The magnolia had unfolded a few more sculptural flowers; the view was undisturbed.

It was hard for Mrs. Manstey to breathe; each moment it grew more difficult. She tried to make them open the window, but they would not understand. If she could have tasted the air, sweet with the penetrating ailanthus savor, it would have eased her; but the view at least was there—the spire was golden now, the heavens had warmed from pearl to blue, day was alight from east to west, even the magnolia had caught the sun.

Mrs. Manstey's head fell back and smiling she died.

That day the building of the extension was resumed.

THE END

THE BOLTED DOOR

As first published in Scribner's Magazine, March 1909

CHAPTER I

Hubert Granice, pacing the length of his pleasant lamp-lit library, paused to compare his watch with the clock on the chimney-piece.

Three minutes to eight.

In exactly three minutes Mr. Peter Ascham, of the eminent legal firm of Ascham and Pettilow, would have his punctual hand on the door-bell of the flat. It was a comfort to reflect that Ascham was so punctual—the suspense was beginning to make his host nervous. And the sound of the door-bell would be the beginning of the end—after that there'd be no going back, by God—no going back!

Granice resumed his pacing. Each time he reached the end of the room opposite the door he caught his reflection in the Florentine mirror above the fine old walnut credence he had picked up at Dijon—saw himself spare, quick-moving, carefully brushed and dressed, but furrowed, gray about the temples, with a stoop which he corrected by a spasmodic straightening of the shoulders whenever a glass confronted him: a tired middle-aged man, baffled, beaten, worn out.

As he summed himself up thus for the third or fourth time the door opened and he turned with a thrill of relief to greet his guest. But it was only the man-servant who entered, advancing silently over the mossy surface of the old Turkey rug.

"Mr. Ascham telephones, sir, to say he's unexpectedly detained and can't be here till eight-thirty."

Granice made a curt gesture of annoyance. It was becoming harder and harder for him to control these reflexes. He turned on his heel, tossing to the servant over his shoulder: "Very good. Put off dinner."

Down his spine he felt the man's injured stare. Mr. Granice had always been so mild-spoken to his people—no doubt the odd change in his manner had already been noticed and discussed below stairs. And very likely they suspected the cause. He stood drumming on the writing-table till he heard the servant go out; then he threw himself into a chair, propping his elbows on the table and resting his chin on his locked hands.

Another half hour alone with it!

He wondered irritably what could have detained his guest. Some professional matter, no doubt—the punctilious lawyer would have allowed nothing less to interfere with a dinner engagement, more especially since Granice, in his note, had said: "I shall want a little business chat afterward."

But what professional matter could have come up at that unprofessional hour? Perhaps some other soul in misery had called on the lawyer; and, after all, Granice's note had given no hint of his own need! No doubt Ascham thought he merely wanted to make another change in his will. Since he had come into his little property, ten years earlier, Granice had been perpetually tinkering with his will.

Suddenly another thought pulled him up, sending a flush to his sallow temples. He remembered a word he had tossed to the lawyer some six weeks earlier, at the Century Club. "Yes—my play's as good as taken. I shall be calling on you soon to go over the contract. Those theatrical chaps are so slippery—I won't trust anybody but you to tie the knot for me!" That, of course, was what Ascham would think he was wanted for. Granice, at the idea, broke into an audible laugh—a queer stage-laugh, like the cackle of a baffled villain in a melodrama. The absurdity, the unnaturalness of the sound abashed him, and he compressed his lips angrily. Would he take to soliloquy next?

He lowered his arms and pulled open the upper drawer of the writing-table. In the right-hand corner lay a thick manuscript, bound in paper folders, and tied with a string beneath which a letter had been slipped. Next to the manuscript was a small revolver. Granice stared a moment at these oddly associated objects; then he took the letter from under the string and slowly began to open it. He had known he should do so from the moment his hand touched the drawer. Whenever his eye fell on that letter some relentless force compelled him to re-read it.

It was dated about four weeks back, under the letter-head of "The Diversity Theatre."

"MY DEAR MR. GRANICE:

"I have given the matter my best consideration for the last month, and it's no use—the play won't do. I have talked it over with Miss Melrose—and you know there isn't a gamer artist on our stage—and I regret to tell you she feels just as I do about it. It isn't the poetry that scares her—or me either. We both want to do all we can to help along the poetic drama—we believe the public's ready for it, and we're willing to take a big financial risk in order to be the first to give them what they want. BUT WE DON'T BELIEVE THEY COULD BE MADE TO WANT THIS. The fact is, there isn't enough drama in your play to the allowance of poetry—the thing drags all through. You've got a big idea, but it's not out of swaddling clothes.

"If this was your first play I'd say: TRY AGAIN. But it has been just the same with all the others you've shown me. And you remember the result of 'The Lee Shore,' where you carried all the expenses of production yourself, and we couldn't fill the theatre for a week. Yet 'The Lee Shore' was a modern problem play—much easier to swing than blank verse. It isn't as if you hadn't tried all kinds—"

Granice folded the letter and put it carefully back into the envelope. Why on earth was he re-reading it, when he knew every phrase in it by heart, when for a month past he had seen it, night after night, stand out in letters of flame against the darkness of his sleepless lids?

"IT HAS BEEN JUST THE SAME WITH ALL THE OTHERS YOU'VE SHOWN ME."

That was the way they dismissed ten years of passionate unremitting work!

"YOU REMEMBER THE RESULT OF 'THE LEE SHORE.'"

Good God—as if he were likely to forget it! He re-lived it all now in a drowning flash: the persistent rejection of the play, his sudden resolve to put it on at his own cost, to spend ten thousand dollars of his inheritance on testing his chance of success—the fever of preparation, the dry-mouthed agony of the "first night," the flat fall, the stupid press, his secret rush to Europe to escape the condolence of his friends!

"IT ISN'T AS IF YOU HADN'T TRIED ALL KINDS."

No—he had tried all kinds: comedy, tragedy, prose and verse, the light curtain-raiser, the short sharp drama, the bourgeois-realistic and the lyrical-romantic—finally deciding that he would no longer "prostitute his talent" to win popularity, but would impose on the public his own theory of art in the form of five acts of blank verse. Yes, he had offered them everything—and always with the same result.

Ten years of it—ten years of dogged work and unrelieved failure. The ten years from forty to fifty—the best ten years of his life! And if one counted the years before, the silent years of dreams, assimilation, preparation—then call it half a man's life-time: half a man's life-time thrown away!

And what was he to do with the remaining half? Well, he had settled that, thank God! He turned and glanced anxiously at the clock. Ten minutes past eight—only ten minutes had been consumed in that stormy rush through his whole past! And he must wait another twenty minutes for Ascham. It was one of the worst symptoms of his case that, in proportion as he had grown to shrink from human company, he dreaded more and more to be alone.... But why the devil was he waiting for Ascham? Why didn't he cut the knot himself? Since he was so unutterably sick of the whole business, why did he have to call in an outsider to rid him of this nightmare of living?

He opened the drawer again and laid his hand on the revolver. It was a small slim ivory toy—just the instrument for a tired sufferer to give himself a "hypodermic" with. Granice raised it slowly in one hand, while with the other he felt under the thin hair at the back of his head, between the ear and the nape. He knew just where to place the muzzle: he had once got a young surgeon to show him. And as he found the spot, and lifted the revolver to it, the inevitable phenomenon occurred. The hand that held the weapon began to shake, the tremor communicated itself to his arm, his heart gave a wild leap which sent up a wave of deadly nausea to his throat, he smelt the powder, he sickened at the crash of the bullet through his skull, and a sweat of fear broke out over his forehead and ran down his quivering face...

He laid away the revolver with an oath and, pulling out a cologne-scented handkerchief, passed it tremulously over his brow and temples. It was no use—he knew he could never do it in that way. His attempts at self-destruction were as futile as his snatches at fame! He couldn't make himself a real life, and he couldn't get rid of the life he had. And that was why he had sent for Ascham to help him...

The lawyer, over the Camembert and Burgundy, began to excuse himself for his delay.

"I didn't like to say anything while your man was about—but the fact is, I was sent for on a rather unusual matter—"

"Oh, it's all right," said Granice cheerfully. He was beginning to feel the usual reaction that food and company produced. It was not any recovered pleasure in life that he felt, but only a deeper withdrawal into himself. It was easier to go on automatically with the social gestures than to uncover to any human eye the abyss within him.

"My dear fellow, it's sacrilege to keep a dinner waiting—especially the production of an artist like yours." Mr. Ascham sipped his Burgundy luxuriously. "But the fact is,

Mrs. Ashgrove sent for me."

Granice raised his head with a quick movement of surprise. For a moment he was shaken out of his self-absorption.

"MRS. ASHGROVE?"

Ascham smiled. "I thought you'd be interested; I know your passion for causes celebres. And this promises to be one. Of course it's out of our line entirely—we never touch criminal cases. But she wanted to consult me as a friend. Ashgrove was a distant connection of my wife's. And, by Jove, it IS a queer case!" The servant re-entered, and Ascham snapped his lips shut.

Would the gentlemen have their coffee in the diningroom?

"No—serve it in the library," said Granice, rising. He led the way back to the curtained confidential room. He was really curious to hear what Ascham had to tell him.

While the coffee and cigars were being served he fidgeted about the library, glancing at his letters—the usual meaningless notes and bills—and picking up the evening paper. As he unfolded it a headline caught his eye.

"ROSE MELROSE WANTS TO
PLAY POETRY.
"THINKS SHE HAS FOUND HER
POET."

He read on with a thumping heart—found the name of a young author he had barely heard of, saw the title of a play, a "poetic drama," dance before his eyes, and dropped the paper, sick, disgusted. It was true, then—she WAS "game"—it was not the manner but the matter she mistrusted!

Granice turned to the servant, who seemed to be purposely lingering. "I shan't need you this evening, Flint. I'll lock up myself."

He fancied the man's acquiescence implied surprise. What was going on, Flint seemed to wonder, that Mr. Granice should want him out of the way? Probably he would find a pretext for coming back to see. Granice suddenly felt himself enveloped in a network of espionage.

As the door closed he threw himself into an armchair and leaned forward to take a light from Ascham's cigar.

"Tell me about Mrs. Ashgrove," he said, seeming to himself to speak stiffly, as if his lips were cracked.

"Mrs. Ashgrove? Well, there's not much to TELL."

"And you couldn't if there were?" Granice smiled.

"Probably not. As a matter of fact, she wanted my advice about her choice of counsel. There was nothing especially confidential in our talk."

"And what's your impression, now you've seen her?"

"My impression is, very distinctly, THAT NOTHING WILL EVER BE KNOWN."

"Ah—?" Granice murmured, puffing at his cigar.

"I'm more and more convinced that whoever poisoned Ashgrove knew his business, and will consequently never be found out. That's a capital cigar you've given me."

"You like it? I get them over from Cuba." Granice examined his own reflectively. "Then you believe in the theory that the clever criminals never ARE caught?"

"Of course I do. Look about you—look back for the last dozen years—none of the big murder problems are ever solved." The lawyer ruminated behind his blue cloud. "Why, take the instance in your own family: I'd forgotten I had an illustration at hand! Take old Joseph Lenman's murder—do you suppose that will ever be explained?"

As the words dropped from Ascham's lips his host looked slowly about the library, and every object in it stared back at him with a stale unescapable familiarity. How sick he was of looking at that room! It was as dull as the face of a wife one has wearied of. He cleared his throat slowly; then he turned his head to the lawyer and said: "I could explain the Lenman murder myself."

Ascham's eye kindled: he shared Granice's interest in criminal cases.

"By Jove! You've had a theory all this time? It's odd you never mentioned it. Go ahead and tell me. There are certain features in the Lenman case not unlike this Ashgrove affair, and your idea may be a help."

Granice paused and his eye reverted instinctively to the table drawer in which the revolver and the manuscript lay side by side. What if he were to try another appeal to Rose

Melrose? Then he looked at the notes and bills on the table, and the horror of taking up again the lifeless routine of life—of performing the same automatic gestures another day—displaced his fleeting vision.

"I haven't a theory. I KNOW who murdered Joseph Lenman."

Ascham settled himself comfortably in his chair, prepared for enjoyment.

"You KNOW? Well, who did?" he laughed.

"I did," said Granice, rising.

He stood before Ascham, and the lawyer lay back staring up at him. Then he broke into another laugh.

"Why, this is glorious! You murdered him, did you? To inherit his money, I suppose? Better and better! Go on, my boy! Unbosom yourself! Tell me all about it! Confession is good for the soul."

Granice waited till the lawyer had shaken the last peal of laughter from his throat; then he repeated doggedly: "I murdered him."

The two men looked at each other for a long moment, and this time Ascham did not laugh.

"Granice!"

"I murdered him—to get his money, as you say."

There was another pause, and Granice, with a vague underlying sense of amusement, saw his guest's look change from pleasantry to apprehension.

"What's the joke, my dear fellow? I fail to see."

"It's not a joke. It's the truth. I murdered him." He had spoken painfully at first, as if there were a knot in his throat; but each time he repeated the words he found they were easier to say.

Ascham laid down his extinct cigar.

"What's the matter? Aren't you well? What on earth are you driving at?"

"I'm perfectly well. But I murdered my cousin, Joseph Lenman, and I want it known that I murdered him."

"YOU WANT IT KNOWN?"

"Yes. That's why I sent for you. I'm sick of living, and when I try to kill myself I funk it." He spoke quite naturally now, as if the knot in his throat had been untied.

"Good Lord—good Lord," the lawyer gasped.

"But I suppose," Granice continued, "there's no doubt this would be murder in the first degree? I'm sure of the chair if I own up?"

Ascham drew a long breath; then he said slowly: "Sit down, Granice. Let's talk."

CHAPTER II

Granice told his story simply, connectedly.

He began by a quick survey of his early years—the years of drudgery and privation. His father, a charming man who could never say "no," had so signally failed to say it on certain essential occasions that when he died he left an illegitimate family and a mortgaged estate. His lawful kin found themselves hanging over a gulf of debt, and young Granice, to support his mother and sister, had to leave Harvard and bury himself at eighteen in a broker's office. He loathed his work, and he was always poor, always worried and in ill-health. A few years later his mother died, but his sister, an ineffectual neurasthenic, remained on his hands. His own health gave out, and he had to go away for six months, and work harder than ever when he came back. He had no knack for business, no head for figures, no dimmest insight into the mysteries of commerce. He wanted to travel and write—those were his inmost longings. And as the years dragged on, and he neared middle-age without making any more money, or acquiring any firmer health, a sick despair possessed him. He tried writing, but he always came home from the office so tired that his brain could not work. For half the year he did not reach his dim up-town flat till after dark, and could only "brush up" for dinner, and afterward lie on the lounge with his pipe, while his sister droned through the evening paper. Sometimes he spent an evening at the theatre; or he dined out, or, more rarely, strayed off with an acquaintance or two in quest of what is known as "pleasure." And in summer, when he and Kate went to the sea-side for a month, he dozed through the days in utter weariness. Once he fell in love with a charming girl—but what had he to offer her, in God's name? She seemed to like him, and in common decency he had to drop out of the running. Apparently no one replaced him, for she never married, but grew stoutish, grayish, philanthropic—yet how sweet she had been when he had first kissed her! One more wasted life, he reflected...

But the stage had always been his master-passion. He would have sold his soul for the time and freedom to write plays! It was IN HIM—he could not remember when it had not been his deepest-seated instinct. As the years passed it became a morbid, a relentless obsession—yet with every year the material conditions were more and more against it. He felt himself growing middle-aged, and he watched the reflection of the process in his sister's wasted face. At eighteen she had been pretty, and as full of enthusiasm as he. Now she was sour, trivial, insignificant—she had missed her chance of life. And she had no resources, poor creature, was fashioned simply for the primitive functions she had been denied the chance to fulfil! It exasperated him to think of it—and to reflect that even now a little travel, a little health, a little money, might transform her, make her young and desirable... The chief fruit of his experience was that there is no such fixed state as age or youth—there is only health as against sickness, wealth as against poverty; and age or youth as the outcome of the lot one draws.

At this point in his narrative Granice stood up, and went to lean against the mantel-piece, looking down at Ascham, who had not moved from his seat, or changed his attitude of rigid fascinated attention.

"Then came the summer when we went to Wrenfield to be near old Lenman—my mother's cousin, as you know. Some of the family always mounted guard over him—generally a niece or so. But that year they were all scattered, and one of the nieces offered to lend us her cottage if we'd relieve her of duty for two months. It was a nuisance for me, of course, for Wrenfield is two hours from town; but my mother, who was a slave to family observances, had always been good to the old man, so it was natural we should be called on—and there was the saving of rent and the good air for Kate. So we went.

"You never knew Joseph Lenman? Well, picture to yourself an amoeba or some primitive organism of that sort, under a Titan's microscope. He was large, undifferentiated, inert—since I could remember him he had done nothing but take his temperature and read the Churchman. Oh, and cultivate melons—that was his hobby. Not vulgar, out-of-door melons—his were grown under glass. He had miles of it at Wrenfield—his big kitchen-garden was surrounded by blinking battalions of green-houses. And in nearly all of them melons were grown—early melons and late, French, English, domestic—dwarf melons and monsters: every shape, colour and variety. They were petted and nursed like children—a staff of trained attendants waited on them. I'm not sure they didn't have a doctor to take their temperature—at any rate the place was full of thermometers. And they didn't sprawl on the ground like ordinary melons; they were trained against the glass like nectarines, and each melon hung in a net which sustained its weight and left it free on all sides to the sun and air...

"It used to strike me sometimes that old Lenman was just like one of his own melons—the pale-fleshed English kind. His life, apathetic and motionless, hung in a net of gold, in an equable warm ventilated atmosphere, high above sordid earthly worries. The cardinal rule of his existence was not to let himself be 'worried.'... I remember his advising me to try it myself, one day when I spoke to him about Kate's bad health, and her need of a change. 'I never let myself worry,' he said complacently. 'It's the worst thing for the liver—and you look to me as if you had a liver. Take my advice and be cheerful. You'll make yourself happier and others too.' And all he had to do was to write a cheque, and send the poor girl off for a holiday!

"The hardest part of it was that the money half-belonged to

us already. The old skin-flint only had it for life, in trust for us and the others. But his life was a good deal sounder than mine or Kate's—and one could picture him taking extra care of it for the joke of keeping us waiting. I always felt that the sight of our hungry eyes was a tonic to him.

"Well, I tried to see if I couldn't reach him through his vanity. I flattered him, feigned a passionate interest in his melons. And he was taken in, and used to discourse on them by the hour. On fine days he was driven to the green-houses in his pony-chair, and waddled through them, prodding and leering at the fruit, like a fat Turk in his seraglio. When he bragged to me of the expense of growing them I was reminded of a hideous old Lothario bragging of what his pleasures cost. And the resemblance was completed by the fact that he couldn't eat as much as a mouthful of his melons—had lived for years on buttermilk and toast. 'But, after all, it's my only hobby—why shouldn't I indulge it?' he said sentimentally. As if I'd ever been able to indulge any of mine! On the keep of those melons Kate and I could have lived like gods...

"One day toward the end of the summer, when Kate was too unwell to drag herself up to the big house, she asked me to go and spend the afternoon with cousin Joseph. It was a lovely soft September afternoon—a day to lie under a Roman stone-pine, with one's eyes on the sky, and let the cosmic harmonies rush through one. Perhaps the vision was suggested by the fact that, as I entered cousin Joseph's hideous black walnut library, I passed one of the under-gardeners, a handsome full-throated Italian, who dashed out in such a hurry that he nearly knocked me down. I remember thinking it queer that the fellow, whom I had often seen about the melon-houses, did not bow to me, or even seem to see me.

"Cousin Joseph sat in his usual seat, behind the darkened windows, his fat hands folded on his protuberant waistcoat, the last number of the Churchman at his elbow, and near it, on a huge dish, a fat melon—the fattest melon I'd ever seen. As I looked at it I pictured the ecstasy of contemplation from which I must have roused him, and congratulated myself on finding him in such a mood, since I had made up my mind to ask him a favour. Then I noticed that his face, instead of looking as calm as an egg-shell, was distorted and whimpering—and without stopping to greet me he pointed passionately to the melon.

"'Look at it, look at it—did you ever see such a beauty? Such firmness—roundness—such delicious smoothness to the touch?' It was as if he had said 'she' instead of 'it,' and when he put out his senile hand and touched the melon I positively had to look the other way.

"Then he told me what had happened. The Italian under-gardener, who had been specially recommended for the melon-houses—though it was against my cousin's principles to employ a Papist—had been assigned to the care of the monster: for it had revealed itself, early in its existence, as destined to become a monster, to surpass its plumpest, pulpiest sisters, carry off prizes at agricultural shows, and be photographed and celebrated in every gardening paper in the land. The Italian had done well—seemed to have a sense of responsibility. And that very morning he had been ordered to pick the melon, which was to be shown next day at the county fair, and to bring it in for Mr. Lenman to gaze on its blonde virginity. But in picking it, what had the damned scoundrelly Jesuit done but drop it—drop it crash on the sharp spout of a watering-pot, so that it received a deep gash in its firm pale rotundity, and was henceforth but a bruised, ruined, fallen melon?

"The old man's rage was fearful in its impotence—he shook, spluttered and strangled with it. He had just had the Italian up and had sacked him on the spot, without wages or character—had threatened to have him arrested if he was ever caught prowling about Wrenfield. 'By God, and I'll do it—I'll write to Washington—I'll have the pauper scoundrel deported! I'll show him what money can do!' As likely as not there was some murderous Black-hand business under it—it would be found that the fellow was a member of a 'gang.' Those Italians would murder you for a quarter. He meant to have the police look into it... And then he grew frightened at his own excitement. 'But I must calm myself,' he said. He took his temperature, rang for his drops, and turned to the Churchman. He had been reading an article on Nestorianism when the melon was brought in. He asked me to go on with it, and I read to him for an hour, in the dim close room, with a fat fly buzzing stealthily about the fallen melon.

"All the while one phrase of the old man's buzzed in my brain like the fly about the melon. 'I'LL SHOW HIM WHAT MONEY CAN DO!' Good heaven! If I could but show the old man! If I could make him see his power of giving happiness as a new outlet for his monstrous egotism! I tried to tell him something about my situation and Kate's—spoke of my ill-health, my unsuccessful drudgery, my longing to write, to make myself a name—I stammered out an entreaty for a loan. 'I can guarantee to repay you, sir—I've a half-written play as security...'

"I shall never forget his glassy stare. His face had grown as smooth as an egg-shell again—his eyes peered over his fat cheeks like sentinels over a slippery rampart.

"'A half-written play—a play of YOURS as security?' He looked at me almost fearfully, as if detecting the first symptoms of insanity. 'Do you understand anything of business?' he enquired mildly. I laughed and answered: 'No, not much.'

"He leaned back with closed lids. 'All this excitement has been too much for me,' he said. 'If you'll excuse me, I'll prepare for my nap.' And I stumbled out of the room, blindly, like the Italian."

Granice moved away from the mantel-piece, and walked across to the tray set out with decanters and soda-water. He poured himself a tall glass of soda-water, emptied it, and glanced at Ascham's dead cigar.

"Better light another," he suggested.

The lawyer shook his head, and Granice went on with his tale. He told of his mounting obsession—how the murderous impulse had waked in him on the instant of his cousin's refusal, and he had muttered to himself: "By God, if you won't, I'll make you." He spoke more tranquilly as the narrative proceeded, as though his rage had died down once the resolve to act on it was taken. He applied his whole mind to the question of how the old man was to be "disposed of." Suddenly he remembered the outcry: "Those Italians will murder you for a quarter!" But no definite project presented itself: he simply waited for an inspiration.

Granice and his sister moved to town a day or two after the incident of the melon. But the cousins, who had returned, kept them informed of the old man's condition. One day, about three weeks later, Granice, on getting home, found Kate excited over a report from Wrenfield. The Italian had been there again—had somehow slipped into the house, made his way up to the library, and "used threatening language." The house-keeper found cousin Joseph gasping, the whites of his eyes showing "something awful." The doctor was sent for, and the attack warded off; and the police had ordered the Italian from the neighbourhood.

But cousin Joseph, thereafter, languished, had "nerves," and lost his taste for toast and butter-milk. The doctor called in a colleague, and the consultation amused and excited the old man—he became once more an important figure. The medical men reassured the family—too completely!— and to the patient they recommended a more varied diet: advised him to take whatever "tempted him." And so one day, tremulously, prayerfully, he decided on a tiny bit of melon. It was brought up with ceremony, and consumed in the presence of the house-keeper and a hovering cousin; and twenty minutes later he was dead...

"But you remember the circumstances," Granice went on; "how suspicion turned at once on the Italian? In spite of the hint the police had given him he had been seen hanging about the house since 'the scene.' It was said that he had tender relations with the kitchen-maid, and the rest seemed easy to explain. But when they looked round to ask him for the explanation he was gone—gone clean out of sight. He had been 'warned' to leave Wrenfield, and he had taken the warning so to heart that no one ever laid eyes on him again."

Granice paused. He had dropped into a chair opposite the lawyer's, and he sat for a moment, his head thrown back, looking about the familiar room. Everything in it had grown grimacing and alien, and each strange insistent object seemed craning forward from its place to hear him.

"It was I who put the stuff in the melon," he said. "And I don't want you to think I'm sorry for it. This isn't 'remorse,' understand. I'm glad the old skin-flint is dead—I'm glad the others have their money. But mine's no use to me any more. My sister married miserably, and died. And I've never had what I wanted."

Ascham continued to stare; then he said: "What on earth was your object, then?"

"Why, to GET what I wanted—what I fancied was in reach! I wanted change, rest, LIFE, for both of us—wanted, above all, for myself, the chance to write! I travelled, got back my health, and came home to tie myself up to my work. And I've slaved at it steadily for ten years without reward—without the most distant hope of success! Nobody will look at my stuff. And now I'm fifty, and I'm beaten, and I know it." His chin dropped forward on his breast. "I want to chuck the whole business," he ended.

CHAPTER III

It was after midnight when Ascham left.

His hand on Granice's shoulder, as he turned to go—
"District Attorney be hanged; see a doctor, see a doctor!" he
had cried; and so, with an exaggerated laugh, had pulled on
his coat and departed.

Granice turned back into the library. It had never occurred
to him that Ascham would not believe his story. For three
hours he had explained, elucidated, patiently and painfully
gone over every detail—but without once breaking down
the iron incredulity of the lawyer's eye.

At first Ascham had feigned to be convinced—but that,
as Granice now perceived, was simply to get him to expose
himself, to entrap him into contradictions. And when the
attempt failed, when Granice triumphantly met and refuted
each disconcerting question, the lawyer dropped the mask
suddenly, and said with a good-humoured laugh: "By Jove,
Granice you'll write a successful play yet. The way you've
worked this all out is a marvel."

Granice swung about furiously—that last sneer about
the play inflamed him. Was all the world in a conspiracy to
deride his failure?

"I did it, I did it," he muttered sullenly, his rage spending
itself against the impenetrable surface of the other's mockery;
and Ascham answered with a smile: "Ever read any of those

books on hallucination? I've got a fairly good medico-legal library. I could send you one or two if you like..."

Left alone, Granice cowered down in the chair before his writing-table. He understood that Ascham thought him off his head.

"Good God—what if they all think me crazy?"

The horror of it broke out over him in a cold sweat—he sat there and shook, his eyes hidden in his icy hands. But gradually, as he began to rehearse his story for the thousandth time, he saw again how incontrovertible it was, and felt sure that any criminal lawyer would believe him.

"That's the trouble—Ascham's not a criminal lawyer. And then he's a friend. What a fool I was to talk to a friend! Even if he did believe me, he'd never let me see it—his instinct would be to cover the whole thing up... But in that case—if he DID believe me—he might think it a kindness to get me shut up in an asylum..." Granice began to tremble again. "Good heaven! If he should bring in an expert—one of those damned alienists! Ascham and Pettilow can do anything—their word always goes. If Ascham drops a hint that I'd better be shut up, I'll be in a strait-jacket by to-morrow! And he'd do it from the kindest motives—be quite right to do it if he thinks I'm a murderer!"

The vision froze him to his chair. He pressed his fists to his bursting temples and tried to think. For the first time he hoped that Ascham had not believed his story.

"But he did—he did! I can see it now—I noticed what a queer eye he cocked at me. Good God, what shall I do—what shall I do?"

He started up and looked at the clock. Half-past one. What if Ascham should think the case urgent, rout out an alienist, and come back with him? Granice jumped to his feet, and his sudden gesture brushed the morning paper from the table. Mechanically he stooped to pick it up, and the movement started a new train of association.

He sat down again, and reached for the telephone book in the rack by his chair.

"Give me three-o-ten... yes."

The new idea in his mind had revived his flagging energy. He would act—act at once. It was only by thus planning ahead, committing himself to some unavoidable line of conduct, that he could pull himself through the meaningless days. Each time he reached a fresh decision it was like coming out of a foggy weltering sea into a calm harbour with lights. One of the queerest phases of his long agony was the intense relief produced by these momentary lulls.

"That the office of the Investigator? Yes? Give me Mr. Denver, please... Hallo, Denver... Yes, Hubert Granice.... Just caught you? Going straight home? Can I come and see you... yes, now... have a talk? It's rather urgent... yes, might give you some first-rate 'copy.'... All right!" He hung up the receiver with a laugh. It had been a happy thought to call up the editor of the Investigator—Robert Denver was the very man he needed...

Granice put out the lights in the library—it was odd how the automatic gestures persisted!—went into the hall, put on his hat and overcoat, and let himself out of the flat. In the hall, a sleepy elevator boy blinked at him and then dropped his head on his folded arms. Granice passed out into the street. At the corner of Fifth Avenue he hailed a crawling cab, and called out an up-town address. The long thoroughfare stretched before him, dim and deserted, like an ancient avenue of tombs. But from Denver's house a friendly beam fell on the pavement; and as Granice sprang from his cab the editor's electric turned the corner.

The two men grasped hands, and Denver, feeling for his latch-key, ushered Granice into the brightly-lit hall.

"Disturb me? Not a bit. You might have, at ten to-morrow morning... but this is my liveliest hour... you know my habits of old."

Granice had known Robert Denver for fifteen years— watched his rise through all the stages of journalism to the Olympian pinnacle of the Investigator's editorial office. In the thick-set man with grizzling hair there were few traces left of the hungry-eyed young reporter who, on his way home in the small hours, used to "bob in" on Granice, while the latter sat grinding at his plays. Denver had to pass Granice's flat on the way to his own, and it became a habit, if he saw a light in the window, and Granice's shadow against the blind, to go in, smoke a pipe, and discuss the universe.

"Well—this is like old times—a good old habit reversed." The editor smote his visitor genially on the shoulder. "Reminds me of the nights when I used to rout you out... How's the play, by the way? There IS a play, I suppose? It's as safe to ask you that as to say to some men: 'How's the baby?'"

Denver laughed good-naturedly, and Granice thought how thick and heavy he had grown. It was evident, even to Granice's tortured nerves, that the words had not been uttered in malice—and the fact gave him a new measure of his insignificance. Denver did not even know that he had been a failure! The fact hurt more than Ascham's irony.

"Come in—come in." The editor led the way into a small cheerful room, where there were cigars and decanters. He pushed an arm-chair toward his visitor, and dropped into another with a comfortable groan.

"Now, then—help yourself. And let's hear all about it."

He beamed at Granice over his pipe-bowl, and the latter, lighting his cigar, said to himself: "Success makes men comfortable, but it makes them stupid."

Then he turned, and began: "Denver, I want to tell you—"

The clock ticked rhythmically on the mantel-piece. The little room was gradually filled with drifting blue layers of smoke, and through them the editor's face came and went like the moon through a moving sky. Once the hour struck—then the rhythmical ticking began again. The atmosphere grew denser and heavier, and beads of perspiration began to roll from Granice's forehead.

"Do you mind if I open the window?"

"No. It IS stuffy in here. Wait—I'll do it myself." Denver pushed down the upper sash, and returned to his chair. "Well—go on," he said, filling another pipe. His composure exasperated Granice.

"There's no use in my going on if you don't believe me."

The editor remained unmoved. "Who says I don't believe you? And how can I tell till you've finished?"

Granice went on, ashamed of his outburst. "It was simple enough, as you'll see. From the day the old man said to me, 'Those Italians would murder you for a quarter,' I dropped everything and just worked at my scheme. It struck me at once that I must find a way of getting to Wrenfield and back in a night—and that led to the idea of a motor. A motor—that never occurred to you? You wonder where I got the money, I suppose. Well, I had a thousand or so put by, and I nosed around till I found what I wanted—a second-hand racer. I knew how to drive a car, and I tried the thing and found it was all right. Times were bad, and I bought it for my price, and stored it away. Where? Why, in one of those no-questions-asked garages where they keep motors that are not for family use. I had a lively cousin who had put me up to that dodge, and I looked about till I found a queer hole where they took in my car like a baby in a foundling asylum... Then I practiced running to Wrenfield and back in a night. I knew the way pretty well, for I'd done it often with the same lively cousin—and in the small hours, too. The distance is over ninety miles, and on the third trial I did it under two hours. But my arms were so lame that I could hardly get dressed the next morning...

"Well, then came the report about the Italian's threats, and I saw I must act at once... I meant to break into the old man's room, shoot him, and get away again. It was a big risk, but I thought I could manage it. Then we heard that he was ill—that there'd been a consultation. Perhaps the fates were going to do it for me! Good Lord, if that could only be!..."

Granice stopped and wiped his forehead: the open window did not seem to have cooled the room.

"Then came word that he was better; and the day after, when I came up from my office, I found Kate laughing over the news that he was to try a bit of melon. The house-keeper had just telephoned her—all Wrenfield was in a flutter. The doctor himself had picked out the melon, one of the little French ones that are hardly bigger than a large tomato—and the patient was to eat it at his breakfast the next morning.

"In a flash I saw my chance. It was a bare chance, no more. But I knew the ways of the house—I was sure the melon would be brought in over night and put in the pantry ice-box. If there were only one melon in the ice-box I could be fairly sure it was the one I wanted. Melons didn't lie around loose in that house—every one was known, numbered, catalogued. The old man was beset by the dread that the servants would eat them, and he took a hundred mean precautions to prevent it. Yes, I felt pretty sure of my melon... and poisoning was much safer than shooting. It would have been the devil and all to get into the old man's bedroom without his rousing the house; but I ought to be able to break into the pantry without much trouble.

"It was a cloudy night, too—everything served me. I dined quietly, and sat down at my desk. Kate had one of her usual headaches, and went to bed early. As soon as she was gone I slipped out. I had got together a sort of disguise—red beard and queer-looking ulster. I shoved them into a bag, and went round to the garage. There was no one there but a half-drunken machinist whom I'd never seen before. That served me, too. They were always changing machinists, and this new fellow didn't even bother to ask if the car belonged to me. It was a very easy-going place...

"Well, I jumped in, ran up Broadway, and let the car go as soon as I was out of Harlem. Dark as it was, I could trust myself to strike a sharp pace. In the shadow of a wood I stopped a second and got into the beard and ulster. Then away again—it was just eleven-thirty when I got to Wrenfield.

"I left the car in a dark lane behind the Lenman place, and slipped through the kitchen-garden. The melon-houses winked at me through the dark—I remember thinking that they knew what I wanted to know.... By the stable a dog came out growling—but he nosed me out, jumped on me, and went back... The house was as dark as the grave. I knew everybody went to bed by ten. But there might be a prowling servant—the kitchen-maid might have come down to let in her Italian. I had to risk that, of course. I crept around by the back door and hid in the shrubbery. Then I listened. It was all as silent as death. I crossed over to the house, pried open the pantry window and climbed in. I had a little electric lamp in my pocket, and shielding it with my cap I groped my way to the ice-box, opened it—and there was the little French melon... only one.

"I stopped to listen—I was quite cool. Then I pulled out my bottle of stuff and my syringe, and gave each section of the melon a hypodermic. It was all done inside of three minutes—at ten minutes to twelve I was back in the car. I got out of the lane as quietly as I could, struck a back road that skirted the village, and let the car out as soon as I was beyond the last houses. I only stopped once on the way in, to drop the beard and ulster into a pond. I had a big stone ready to weight them with and they went down plump, like a dead body—and at two o'clock I was back at my desk."

Granice stopped speaking and looked across the

smoke-fumes at his listener; but Denver's face remained inscrutable.

At length he said: "Why did you want to tell me this?"

The question startled Granice. He was about to explain, as he had explained to Ascham; but suddenly it occurred to him that if his motive had not seemed convincing to the lawyer it would carry much less weight with Denver. Both were successful men, and success does not understand the subtle agony of failure. Granice cast about for another reason.

"Why, I—the thing haunts me... remorse, I suppose you'd call it..."

Denver struck the ashes from his empty pipe.

"Remorse? Bosh!" he said energetically.

Granice's heart sank. "You don't believe in— REMORSE?"

"Not an atom: in the man of action. The mere fact of your talking of remorse proves to me that you're not the man to have planned and put through such a job."

Granice groaned. "Well—I lied to you about remorse. I've never felt any."

Denver's lips tightened sceptically about his freshly-filled pipe. "What was your motive, then? You must have had one."

"I'll tell you—" And Granice began again to rehearse the story of his failure, of his loathing for life. "Don't say you don't believe me this time... that this isn't a real reason!" he stammered out piteously as he ended.

Denver meditated. "No, I won't say that. I've seen too many queer things. There's always a reason for wanting to get out of life—the wonder is that we find so many for staying in!" Granice's heart grew light. "Then you DO believe me?" he faltered.

"Believe that you're sick of the job? Yes. And that you haven't the nerve to pull the trigger? Oh, yes—that's easy enough, too. But all that doesn't make you a murderer—though I don't say it proves you could never have been one."

"I HAVE been one, Denver—I swear to you."

"Perhaps." He meditated. "Just tell me one or two things."

"Oh, go ahead. You won't stump me!" Granice heard himself say with a laugh.

"Well—how did you make all those trial trips without exciting your sister's curiosity? I knew your night habits pretty well at that time, remember. You were very seldom out late. Didn't the change in your ways surprise her?"

"No; because she was away at the time. She went to pay several visits in the country soon after we came back from Wrenfield, and was only in town for a night or two before—before I did the job."

"And that night she went to bed early with a headache?"

"Yes—blinding. She didn't know anything when she had that kind. And her room was at the back of the flat."

Denver again meditated. "And when you got back—she didn't hear you? You got in without her knowing it?"

"Yes. I went straight to my work—took it up at the word where I'd left off—WHY, DENVER, DON'T YOU REMEMBER?" Granice suddenly, passionately interjected.

"Remember—?"

"Yes; how you found me—when you looked in that morning, between two and three... your usual hour...?"

"Yes," the editor nodded.

Granice gave a short laugh. "In my old coat—with my pipe: looked as if I'd been working all night, didn't I? Well, I hadn't been in my chair ten minutes!"

Denver uncrossed his legs and then crossed them again. "I didn't know whether YOU remembered that."

"What?"

"My coming in that particular night—or morning."

Granice swung round in his chair. "Why, man alive! That's why I'm here now. Because it was you who spoke for me at the inquest, when they looked round to see what all the old man's heirs had been doing that night—you who testified to having dropped in and found me at my desk as usual.... I thought THAT would appeal to your journalistic sense if nothing else would!"

Denver smiled. "Oh, my journalistic sense is still susceptible enough—and the idea's picturesque, I grant you: asking the man who proved your alibi to establish your guilt."

"That's it—that's it!" Granice's laugh had a ring of triumph.

"Well, but how about the other chap's testimony—I mean that young doctor: what was his name? Ned Ranney. Don't you remember my testifying that I'd met him at the elevated station, and told him I was on my way to smoke a pipe with you, and his saying: 'All right; you'll find him in. I passed the house two hours ago, and saw his shadow against the blind, as usual.' And the lady with the toothache in the flat across the way: she corroborated his statement, you remember."

"Yes; I remember."

"Well, then?"

"Simple enough. Before starting I rigged up a kind of mannikin with old coats and a cushion—something to cast a shadow on the blind. All you fellows were used to seeing my shadow there in the small hours—I counted on that, and knew you'd take any vague outline as mine."

"Simple enough, as you say. But the woman with the toothache saw the shadow move—you remember she said she saw you sink forward, as if you'd fallen asleep."

"Yes; and she was right. It DID move. I suppose some extra-heavy dray must have jolted by the flimsy building—at any rate, something gave my mannikin a jar, and when I came back he had sunk forward, half over the table."

There was a long silence between the two men. Granice, with a throbbing heart, watched Denver refill his pipe.

The editor, at any rate, did not sneer and flout him. After all, journalism gave a deeper insight than the law into the fantastic possibilities of life, prepared one better to allow for the incalculableness of human impulses.

"Well?" Granice faltered out.

Denver stood up with a shrug. "Look here, man—what's wrong with you? Make a clean breast of it! Nerves gone to smash? I'd like to take you to see a chap I know—an ex-prize-fighter—who's a wonder at pulling fellows in your state out of their hole—"

"Oh, oh—" Granice broke in. He stood up also, and the two men eyed each other. "You don't believe me, then?"

"This yarn—how can I? There wasn't a flaw in your alibi."

"But haven't I filled it full of them now?"

Denver shook his head. "I might think so if I hadn't happened to know that you WANTED to. There's the hitch, don't you see?"

Granice groaned. "No, I didn't. You mean my wanting to be found guilty—?"

"Of course! If somebody else had accused you, the story might have been worth looking into. As it is, a child could have invented it. It doesn't do much credit to your ingenuity."

Granice turned sullenly toward the door. What was the use of arguing? But on the threshold a sudden impulse drew him back. "Look here, Denver—I daresay you're right. But will you do just one thing to prove it? Put my statement in the Investigator, just as I've made it. Ridicule it as much as you like. Only give the other fellows a chance at it—men who don't know anything about me. Set them talking and looking about. I don't care a damn whether YOU believe me—what I want is to convince the Grand Jury! I oughtn't to have come to a man who knows me—your cursed incredulity is infectious. I don't put my case well, because I know in advance it's discredited, and I almost end by not believing it myself. That's why I can't convince YOU. It's a vicious circle." He laid a hand on Denver's arm. "Send a stenographer, and put my statement in the paper."

But Denver did not warm to the idea. "My dear fellow, you seem to forget that all the evidence was pretty thoroughly sifted at the time, every possible clue followed up. The public would have been ready enough then to believe that you murdered old Lenman—you or anybody else. All they wanted was a murderer—the most improbable would have served. But your alibi was too confoundedly complete. And nothing you've told me has shaken it." Denver laid his cool hand over the other's burning fingers. "Look here, old fellow, go home and work up a better case—then come in and submit it to the Investigator."

CHAPTER IV

The perspiration was rolling off Granice's forehead. Every few minutes he had to draw out his handkerchief and wipe the moisture from his haggard face.

For an hour and a half he had been talking steadily, putting his case to the District Attorney. Luckily he had a speaking acquaintance with Allonby, and had obtained, without much difficulty, a private audience on the very day after his talk with Robert Denver. In the interval between he had hurried home, got out of his evening clothes, and gone forth again at once into the dreary dawn. His fear of Ascham and the alienist made it impossible for him to remain in his rooms. And it seemed to him that the only way of averting that hideous peril was by establishing, in some sane impartial mind, the proof of his guilt. Even if he had not been so incurably sick of life, the electric chair seemed now the only alternative to the strait-jacket.

As he paused to wipe his forehead he saw the District Attorney glance at his watch. The gesture was significant, and Granice lifted an appealing hand. "I don't expect you to believe me now—but can't you put me under arrest, and have the thing looked into?"

Allonby smiled faintly under his heavy grayish moustache. He had a ruddy face, full and jovial, in which his keen professional eyes seemed to keep watch over impulses not strictly professional.

"Well, I don't know that we need lock you up just yet. But of course I'm bound to look into your statement—"

Granice rose with an exquisite sense of relief. Surely Allonby wouldn't have said that if he hadn't believed him!

"That's all right. Then I needn't detain you. I can be found at any time at my apartment." He gave the address.

The District Attorney smiled again, more openly. "What do you say to leaving it for an hour or two this evening? I'm giving a little supper at Rector's—quiet, little affair, you understand: just Miss Melrose—I think you know her—and a friend or two; and if you'll join us..."

Granice stumbled out of the office without knowing what reply he had made.

He waited for four days—four days of concentrated horror. During the first twenty-four hours the fear of Ascham's alienist dogged him; and as that subsided, it was replaced by the exasperating sense that his avowal had made no impression on the District Attorney. Evidently, if he had been going to look into the case, Allonby would have been heard from before now.... And that mocking invitation to supper showed clearly enough how little the story had impressed him!

Granice was overcome by the futility of any farther attempt to inculpate himself. He was chained to life—a "prisoner of consciousness." Where was it he had read the phrase? Well, he was learning what it meant. In the glaring night-hours, when his brain seemed ablaze, he was visited by a sense of his fixed identity, of his irreducible, inexpugnable SELFNESS, keener, more insidious, more unescapable, than any sensation he had ever known. He had not guessed that the mind was capable of such intricacies of self-realization, of penetrating so deep into its own dark windings. Often he woke from his brief snatches of sleep with the feeling that something material was clinging to him, was on his hands and face, and in his throat—and as his brain cleared he understood that it was the sense of his own loathed personality that stuck to him like some thick viscous substance.

Then, in the first morning hours, he would rise and look out of his window at the awakening activities of the street—at the street-cleaners, the ash-cart drivers, and the other dingy workers flitting hurriedly by through the sallow winter light. Oh, to be one of them—any of them—to take his chance in any of their skins! They were the toilers—the men whose lot was pitied—the victims wept over and ranted about by altruists and economists; and how gladly he would have taken up the load of any one of them, if only he might have shaken off his own! But, no—the iron circle of consciousness held them too: each one was hand-cuffed to his own hideous ego. Why wish to be any one man rather than another? The only absolute good was not to be... And Flint, coming in to draw his bath, would ask if he preferred his eggs scrambled or poached that morning?

On the fifth day he wrote a long urgent letter to Allonby; and for the succeeding two days he had the occupation of waiting for an answer. He hardly stirred from his rooms, in his fear of missing the letter by a moment; but would the District Attorney write, or send a representative: a policeman, a "secret agent," or some other mysterious emissary of the law?

On the third morning Flint, stepping softly—as if, confound it! his master were ill—entered the library where Granice sat behind an unread newspaper, and proferred a card on a tray.

Granice read the name—J. B. Hewson—and underneath, in pencil, "From the District Attorney's office." He started up with a thumping heart, and signed an assent to the servant.

Mr. Hewson was a slight sallow nondescript man of about fifty—the kind of man of whom one is sure to see a specimen in any crowd. "Just the type of the successful detective," Granice reflected as he shook hands with his visitor.

And it was in that character that Mr. Hewson briefly introduced himself. He had been sent by the District Attorney to have "a quiet talk" with Mr. Granice—to ask him to repeat the statement he had made about the Lenman murder.

His manner was so quiet, so reasonable and receptive, that Granice's self-confidence returned. Here was a sensible man—a man who knew his business—it would be easy enough to make HIM see through that ridiculous alibi! Granice offered Mr. Hewson a cigar, and lighting one himself—to prove his coolness—began again to tell his story.

He was conscious, as he proceeded, of telling it better than ever before. Practice helped, no doubt; and his listener's detached, impartial attitude helped still more. He could see that Hewson, at least, had not decided in advance to disbelieve him, and the sense of being trusted made him more lucid and more consecutive. Yes, this time his words would certainly carry conviction...

CHAPTER V

Despairingly, Granice gazed up and down the shabby street. Beside him stood a young man with bright prominent eyes, a smooth but not too smoothly-shaven face, and an Irish smile. The young man's nimble glance followed Granice's.

"Sure of the number, are you?" he asked briskly.

"Oh, yes—it was 104."

"Well, then, the new building has swallowed it up—that's certain."

He tilted his head back and surveyed the half-finished front of a brick and limestone flat-house that reared its flimsy elegance above a row of tottering tenements and stables.

"Dead sure?" he repeated.

"Yes," said Granice, discouraged. "And even if I hadn't been, I know the garage was just opposite Leffler's over there." He pointed across the street to a tumble-down stable with a blotched sign on which the words "Livery and Boarding" were still faintly discernible.

The young man dashed across to the opposite pavement. "Well, that's something—may get a clue there. Leffler's— same name there, anyhow. You remember that name?"

"Yes—distinctly."

Granice had felt a return of confidence since he had enlisted the interest of the Explorer's "smartest" reporter. If there were moments when he hardly believed his own story, there were others when it seemed impossible that every one should not believe it; and young Peter McCarren, peering, listening, questioning, jotting down notes, inspired him with an exquisite sense of security. McCarren had fastened on the case at once, "like a leech," as he phrased it—jumped at it, thrilled to it, and settled down to "draw the last drop of fact from it, and had not let go till he had." No one else had treated Granice in that way—even Allonby's detective had not taken a single note. And though a week had elapsed since the visit of that authorized official, nothing had been heard from the District Attorney's office: Allonby had apparently dropped the matter again. But McCarren wasn't going to drop it—not he! He positively hung on Granice's footsteps. They had spent the greater part of the previous day together, and now they were off again, running down clues.

But at Leffler's they got none, after all. Leffler's was no longer a stable. It was condemned to demolition, and in the respite between sentence and execution it had become a vague place of storage, a hospital for broken-down carriages and carts, presided over by a blear-eyed old woman who knew nothing of Flood's garage across the way—did not even remember what had stood there before the new flat-house began to rise.

"Well—we may run Leffler down somewhere; I've seen harder jobs done," said McCarren, cheerfully noting down the name.

As they walked back toward Sixth Avenue he added, in a less sanguine tone: "I'd undertake now to put the thing through if you could only put me on the track of that cyanide."

Granice's heart sank. Yes—there was the weak spot; he had felt it from the first! But he still hoped to convince McCarren that his case was strong enough without it; and he urged the reporter to come back to his rooms and sum up the facts with him again.

"Sorry, Mr. Granice, but I'm due at the office now. Besides, it'd be no use till I get some fresh stuff to work on. Suppose I call you up tomorrow or next day?"

He plunged into a trolley and left Granice gazing desolately after him.

Two days later he reappeared at the apartment, a shade less jaunty in demeanor.

"Well, Mr. Granice, the stars in their courses are against you, as the bard says. Can't get a trace of Flood, or of Leffler either. And you say you bought the motor through Flood, and sold it through him, too?"

"Yes," said Granice wearily.

"Who bought it, do you know?"

Granice wrinkled his brows. "Why, Flood—yes, Flood himself. I sold it back to him three months later."

"Flood? The devil! And I've ransacked the town for Flood. That kind of business disappears as if the earth had swallowed it."

Granice, discouraged, kept silence.

"That brings us back to the poison," McCarren continued, his note-book out. "Just go over that again, will you?"

And Granice went over it again. It had all been so simple at the time—and he had been so clever in covering up his traces! As soon as he decided on poison he looked about for an acquaintance who manufactured chemicals; and there was Jim Dawes, a Harvard classmate, in the dyeing business—just the man. But at the last moment it occurred to him that suspicion might turn toward so obvious an opportunity, and he decided on a more tortuous course. Another friend, Carrick Venn, a student of medicine whom irremediable ill-health had kept from the practice of his profession, amused his leisure with experiments in physics, for the exercise of which he had set up a simple laboratory. Granice had the habit of dropping in to smoke a cigar with him on Sunday afternoons, and the friends generally sat in Venn's work-shop, at the back of the old family house in Stuyvesant Square. Off this work-shop was the cupboard of supplies, with its row of deadly bottles. Carrick Venn was an original, a man of restless curious tastes, and his place, on a Sunday, was often full of visitors: a cheerful crowd of journalists, scribblers, painters, experimenters in divers forms of expression. Coming and going among so many, it was easy enough to pass unperceived; and one afternoon Granice, arriving before Venn had returned home, found himself alone in the work-shop, and quickly slipping into the cupboard, transferred the drug to his pocket.

But that had happened ten years ago; and Venn, poor fellow, was long since dead of his dragging ailment. His old father was dead, too, the house in Stuyvesant Square had been turned into a boarding-house, and the shifting life of New York had passed its rapid sponge over every trace of their obscure little history. Even the optimistic McCarren seemed to acknowledge the hopelessness of seeking for proof in that direction.

"And there's the third door slammed in our faces." He shut his note-book, and throwing back his head, rested his bright inquisitive eyes on Granice's furrowed face.

"Look here, Mr. Granice—you see the weak spot, don't you?"

The other made a despairing motion. "I see so many!"

"Yes: but the one that weakens all the others. Why the deuce do you want this thing known? Why do you want to put your head into the noose?"

Granice looked at him hopelessly, trying to take the measure of his quick light irreverent mind. No one so full of a cheerful animal life would believe in the craving for death as a sufficient motive; and Granice racked his brain for one more convincing. But suddenly he saw the reporter's face soften, and melt to a naive sentimentalism.

"Mr. Granice—has the memory of it always haunted

you?"

Granice stared a moment, and then leapt at the opening. "That's it—the memory of it... always..."

McCarren nodded vehemently. "Dogged your steps, eh? Wouldn't let you sleep? The time came when you HAD to make a clean breast of it?"

"I had to. Can't you understand?"

The reporter struck his fist on the table. "God, sir! I don't suppose there's a human being with a drop of warm blood in him that can't picture the deadly horrors of remorse—"

The Celtic imagination was aflame, and Granice mutely thanked him for the word. What neither Ascham nor Denver would accept as a conceivable motive the Irish reporter seized on as the most adequate; and, as he said, once one could find a convincing motive, the difficulties of the case became so many incentives to effort.

"Remorse—REMORSE," he repeated, rolling the word under his tongue with an accent that was a clue to the psychology of the popular drama; and Granice, perversely, said to himself: "If I could only have struck that note I should have been running in six theatres at once."

He saw that from that moment McCarren's professional zeal would be fanned by emotional curiosity; and he profited by the fact to propose that they should dine together, and go on afterward to some music-hall or theatre. It was becoming necessary to Granice to feel himself an object of pre-occupation, to find himself in another mind. He took a kind of gray penumbral pleasure in riveting McCarren's attention on his case; and to feign the grimaces of moral anguish became a passionately engrossing game. He had not entered a theatre for months; but he sat out the meaningless performance in rigid tolerance, sustained by the sense of the reporter's observation.

Between the acts, McCarren amused him with anecdotes about the audience: he knew every one by sight, and could lift the curtain from every physiognomy. Granice listened indulgently. He had lost all interest in his kind, but he knew that he was himself the real centre of McCarren's attention, and that every word the latter spoke had an indirect bearing on his own problem.

"See that fellow over there—the little dried-up man in the third row, pulling his moustache? HIS memoirs would be worth publishing," McCarren said suddenly in the last entr'acte.

Granice, following his glance, recognized the detective from Allonby's office. For a moment he had the thrilling sense that he was being shadowed.

"Caesar, if HE could talk—!" McCarren continued. "Know who he is, of course? Dr. John B. Stell, the biggest alienist in the country—"

Granice, with a start, bent again between the heads in front of him. "THAT man—the fourth from the aisle? You're mistaken. That's not Dr. Stell."

McCarren laughed. "Well, I guess I've been in court enough to know Stell when I see him. He testifies in nearly all the big cases where they plead insanity."

A cold shiver ran down Granice's spine, but he repeated obstinately: "That's not Dr. Stell."

"Not Stell? Why, man, I KNOW him. Look—here he comes. If it isn't Stell, he won't speak to me."

The little dried-up man was moving slowly up the aisle. As he neared McCarren he made a slight gesture of recognition.

"How'do, Doctor Stell? Pretty slim show, ain't it?" the reporter cheerfully flung out at him. And Mr. J. B. Hewson, with a nod of amicable assent, passed on.

Granice sat benumbed. He knew he had not been mistaken—the man who had just passed was the same man whom Allonby had sent to see him: a physician disguised as a detective. Allonby, then, had thought him insane, like the others—had regarded his confession as the maundering of a maniac. The discovery froze Granice with horror—he seemed to see the mad-house gaping for him.

"Isn't there a man a good deal like him—a detective named J. B. Hewson?"

But he knew in advance what McCarren's answer would be. "Hewson? J. B. Hewson? Never heard of him. But that was J. B. Stell fast enough—I guess he can be trusted to know himself, and you saw he answered to his name."

CHAPTER VI

Some days passed before Granice could obtain a word with the District Attorney: he began to think that Allonby avoided him.

But when they were face to face Allonby's jovial countenance showed no sign of embarrassment. He waved his visitor to a chair, and leaned across his desk with the encouraging smile of a consulting physician.

Granice broke out at once: "That detective you sent me the other day—"

Allonby raised a deprecating hand.

"—I know: it was Stell the alienist. Why did you do that, Allonby?"

The other's face did not lose its composure. "Because I looked up your story first—and there's nothing in it."

"Nothing in it?" Granice furiously interposed.

"Absolutely nothing. If there is, why the deuce don't you bring me proofs? I know you've been talking to Peter Ascham, and to Denver, and to that little ferret McCarren of the Explorer. Have any of them been able to make out a case for you? No. Well, what am I to do?"

Granice's lips began to tremble. "Why did you play me that trick?"

"About Stell? I had to, my dear fellow: it's part of my business. Stell IS a detective, if you come to that—every doctor is."

The trembling of Granice's lips increased, communicating itself in a long quiver to his facial muscles. He forced a laugh through his dry throat. "Well—and what did he detect?"

"In you? Oh, he thinks it's overwork—overwork and too much smoking. If you look in on him some day at his office he'll show you the record of hundreds of cases like yours, and advise you what treatment to follow. It's one of the commonest forms of hallucination. Have a cigar, all the same."

"But, Allonby, I killed that man!"

The District Attorney's large hand, outstretched on his desk, had an almost imperceptible gesture, and a moment later, as if an answer to the call of an electric bell, a clerk looked in from the outer office.

"Sorry, my dear fellow—lot of people waiting. Drop in on Stell some morning," Allonby said, shaking hands.

McCarren had to own himself beaten: there was absolutely no flaw in the alibi. And since his duty to his journal obviously forbade his wasting time on insoluble mysteries, he ceased to frequent Granice, who dropped back into a deeper isolation. For a day or two after his visit to Allonby he continued to live in dread of Dr. Stell. Why might not Allonby have deceived him as to the alienist's diagnosis? What if he were really being shadowed, not by a police agent but by a mad-doctor? To have the truth out, he suddenly determined to call on Dr. Stell.

The physician received him kindly, and reverted without embarrassment to the conditions of their previous meeting. "We have to do that occasionally, Mr. Granice; it's one of our methods. And you had given Allonby a fright."

Granice was silent. He would have liked to reaffirm his guilt, to produce the fresh arguments which had occurred to him since his last talk with the physician; but he feared his eagerness might be taken for a symptom of derangement, and he affected to smile away Dr. Stell's allusion.

"You think, then, it's a case of brain-fag—nothing more?"

"Nothing more. And I should advise you to knock off tobacco. You smoke a good deal, don't you?"

He developed his treatment, recommending massage, gymnastics, travel, or any form of diversion that did not— that in short—

Granice interrupted him impatiently. "Oh, I loathe all that—and I'm sick of travelling."

"H'm. Then some larger interest—politics, reform, philanthropy? Something to take you out of yourself."

"Yes. I understand," said Granice wearily.

"Above all, don't lose heart. I see hundreds of cases like yours," the doctor added cheerfully from the threshold.

On the doorstep Granice stood still and laughed. Hundreds of cases like his—the case of a man who had committed a murder, who confessed his guilt, and whom no one would believe! Why, there had never been a case like it in the world. What a good figure Stell would have made in a play: the great alienist who couldn't read a man's mind any better than that!

Granice saw huge comic opportunities in the type.

But as he walked away, his fears dispelled, the sense of listlessness returned on him. For the first time since his avowal to Peter Ascham he found himself without an occupation, and understood that he had been carried through the past weeks only by the necessity of constant action. Now his life had once more become a stagnant backwater, and as he stood on the street corner watching the tides of traffic sweep by, he asked himself despairingly how much longer he could endure to float about in the sluggish circle of his consciousness.

The thought of self-destruction recurred to him; but again his flesh recoiled. He yearned for death from other hands, but he could never take it from his own. And, aside from his insuperable physical reluctance, another motive restrained him. He was possessed by the dogged desire to establish the truth of his story. He refused to be swept aside as an irresponsible dreamer—even if he had to kill himself in the end, he would not do so before proving to society that he had deserved death from it.

He began to write long letters to the papers; but after the first had been published and commented on, public curiosity was quelled by a brief statement from the District Attorney's office, and the rest of his communications remained unprinted. Ascham came to see him, and begged him to travel. Robert Denver dropped in, and tried to joke him out of his delusion; till Granice, mistrustful of their motives, began to dread the reappearance of Dr. Stell, and set a guard on his lips. But the words he kept back engendered others and still others in his brain. His inner self became a humming factory of arguments, and he spent long hours reciting and writing down elaborate statements of his crime, which he constantly retouched and developed. Then gradually his activity languished under the lack of an audience, the sense of being buried beneath deepening drifts of indifference. In a passion of resentment he swore that he would prove himself a murderer, even if he had to commit another crime to do it; and for a sleepless night or two the thought flamed red on his darkness. But daylight dispelled it. The determining impulse was lacking and he hated too promiscuously to choose his victim... So he was thrown back on the unavailing struggle to impose the truth of his story. As fast as one channel closed on him he tried to pierce another through the sliding sands of incredulity. But every issue seemed blocked, and the whole human race leagued together to cheat one man of the right to die.

Thus viewed, the situation became so monstrous that he lost his last shred of self-restraint in contemplating it. What if he were really the victim of some mocking experiment, the centre of a ring of holiday-makers jeering at a poor creature in its blind dashes against the solid walls of consciousness? But, no—men were not so uniformly cruel: there were flaws in the close surface of their indifference, cracks of weakness and pity here and there...

Granice began to think that his mistake lay in having appealed to persons more or less familiar with his past, and to whom the visible conformities of his life seemed a final disproof of its one fierce secret deviation. The general tendency was to take for the whole of life the slit seen between the blinders of habit: and in his walk down that narrow vista Granice cut a correct enough figure. To a vision free to follow his whole orbit his story would be more intelligible: it would be easier to convince a chance idler in the street than the trained intelligence hampered by a sense of his antecedents. This idea shot up in him with the tropic luxuriance of each new seed of thought, and he began to walk the streets, and to frequent out-of-the-way chop-houses and bars in his search for the impartial stranger to whom he should disclose himself.

At first every face looked encouragement; but at the crucial moment he always held back. So much was at stake, and it was so essential that his first choice should be decisive. He dreaded stupidity, timidity, intolerance. The imaginative eye, the furrowed brow, were what he sought. He must reveal himself only to a heart versed in the tortuous motions of the human will; and he began to hate the dull benevolence of the average face. Once or twice, obscurely, allusively, he made a beginning—once sitting down at a man's side in a basement chop-house, another day approaching a lounger on an east-side wharf. But in both cases the premonition of failure checked him on the brink of avowal. His dread of being taken for a man in the clutch of a fixed idea gave him an unnatural keenness in reading the expression of his interlocutors, and he had provided himself in advance with a series of verbal alternatives, trap-doors of evasion from the first dart of ridicule or suspicion.

He passed the greater part of the day in the streets, coming home at irregular hours, dreading the silence and orderliness of his apartment, and the critical scrutiny of Flint. His real life was spent in a world so remote from this familiar setting that he sometimes had the mysterious sense of a living metempsychosis, a furtive passage from one identity to another—yet the other as unescapably himself!

One humiliation he was spared: the desire to live never revived in him. Not for a moment was he tempted to a shabby pact with existing conditions. He wanted to die, wanted it with the fixed unwavering desire which alone attains its end. And still the end eluded him! It would not always, of course—he had full faith in the dark star of his destiny. And he could prove it best by repeating his story, persistently and indefatigably, pouring it into indifferent ears, hammering it into dull brains, till at last it kindled a spark, and some one of the careless millions paused, listened, believed...

It was a mild March day, and he had been loitering on the west-side docks, looking at faces. He was becoming an expert in physiognomies: his eagerness no longer made rash darts and awkward recoils. He knew now the face he needed, as clearly as if it had come to him in a vision; and not till he found it would he speak. As he walked eastward through the shabby reeking streets he had a premonition that he should find it that morning. Perhaps it was the promise of spring in the air—certainly he felt calmer than for many days...

He turned into Washington Square, struck across it obliquely, and walked up University Place. Its heterogeneous passers always allured him—they were less hurried than in Broadway, less enclosed and classified than in Fifth Avenue. He walked slowly, watching for his face.

At Union Square he felt a sudden relapse into discouragement, like a votary who has watched too long for a sign from the altar. Perhaps, after all, he should never find his face... The air was languid, and he felt tired. He walked between the bald grass-plots and the twisted trees, making for an empty seat. Presently he passed a bench on which a girl sat alone, and something as definite as the twitch of a cord made him stop before her. He had never dreamed of telling his story to a girl, had hardly looked at the women's faces as they passed. His case was man's work: how could a woman help him? But this girl's face was extraordinary—quiet and wide as a clear evening sky. It suggested a hundred images of space, distance, mystery, like ships he had seen, as a boy, quietly berthed by a familiar wharf, but with the breath of far seas and strange harbours in their shrouds... Certainly this girl would understand. He went up to her quietly, lifting his hat, observing the forms—wishing her to see at once that he was "a gentleman."

"I am a stranger to you," he began, sitting down beside her, "but your face is so extremely intelligent that I feel... I feel it is the face I've waited for... looked for everywhere; and I want to tell you—"

The girl's eyes widened: she rose to her feet. She was escaping him!

In his dismay he ran a few steps after her, and caught her roughly by the arm.

"Here—wait—listen! Oh, don't scream, you fool!" he shouted out.

He felt a hand on his own arm; turned and confronted a policeman. Instantly he understood that he was being arrested, and something hard within him was loosened and ran to tears.

"Ah, you know—you KNOW I'm guilty!"

He was conscious that a crowd was forming, and that the girl's frightened face had disappeared. But what did he care about her face? It was the policeman who had really understood him. He turned and followed, the crowd at his heels...

CHAPTER VII

In the charming place in which he found himself there were so many sympathetic faces that he felt more than ever convinced of the certainty of making himself heard.

It was a bad blow, at first, to find that he had not been arrested for murder; but Ascham, who had come to him at once, explained that he needed rest, and the time to "review" his statements; it appeared that reiteration had made them a little confused and contradictory. To this end he had willingly acquiesced in his removal to a large quiet establishment, with an open space and trees about it, where he had found a number of intelligent companions, some, like himself, engaged in preparing or reviewing statements of their cases, and others ready to lend an interested ear to his own recital.

For a time he was content to let himself go on the tranquil current of this existence; but although his auditors gave him for the most part an encouraging attention, which, in some, went the length of really brilliant and helpful suggestion, he gradually felt a recurrence of his old doubts. Either his hearers were not sincere, or else they had less power to aid him than they boasted. His interminable conferences resulted in nothing, and as the benefit of the long rest made itself felt, it produced an increased mental lucidity which rendered inaction more and more unbearable. At length he discovered that on certain days visitors from the outer world were admitted to his retreat; and he wrote out long and logically constructed relations of his crime, and furtively slipped them into the hands of these messengers of hope.

This occupation gave him a fresh lease of patience, and he now lived only to watch for the visitors' days, and scan the faces that swept by him like stars seen and lost in the rifts of a hurrying sky.

Mostly, these faces were strange and less intelligent than those of his companions. But they represented his last means of access to the world, a kind of subterranean channel on which he could set his "statements" afloat, like paper boats which the mysterious current might sweep out into the open seas of life.

One day, however, his attention was arrested by a familiar contour, a pair of bright prominent eyes, and a chin insufficiently shaved. He sprang up and stood in the path of Peter McCarren.

The journalist looked at him doubtfully, then held out his hand with a startled deprecating, "WHY—?"

"You didn't know me? I'm so changed?" Granice faltered, feeling the rebound of the other's wonder.

"Why, no; but you're looking quieter—smoothed out," McCarren smiled.

"Yes: that's what I'm here for—to rest. And I've taken the opportunity to write out a clearer statement—"

Granice's hand shook so that he could hardly draw the folded paper from his pocket. As he did so he noticed that the reporter was accompanied by a tall man with grave compassionate eyes. It came to Granice in a wild thrill of conviction that this was the face he had waited for...

"Perhaps your friend—he IS your friend?—would glance over it—or I could put the case in a few words if you have time?" Granice's voice shook like his hand. If this chance escaped him he felt that his last hope was gone. McCarren and the stranger looked at each other, and the former glanced at his watch.

"I'm sorry we can't stay and talk it over now, Mr. Granice; but my friend has an engagement, and we're rather pressed—"

Granice continued to proffer the paper. "I'm sorry—I think I could have explained. But you'll take this, at any rate?"

The stranger looked at him gently. "Certainly—I'll take it." He had his hand out. "Good-bye."

"Good-bye," Granice echoed.

He stood watching the two men move away from him through the long light hall; and as he watched them a tear ran down his face. But as soon as they were out of sight he turned and walked hastily toward his room, beginning to hope again, already planning a new statement.

Outside the building the two men stood still, and the journalist's companion looked up curiously at the long monotonous rows of barred windows.

"So that was Granice?"

"Yes—that was Granice, poor devil," said McCarren.

"Strange case! I suppose there's never been one just like it? He's still absolutely convinced that he committed that murder?"

"Absolutely. Yes."

The stranger reflected. "And there was no conceivable ground for the idea? No one could make out how it started? A quiet conventional sort of fellow like that—where do you suppose he got such a delusion? Did you ever get the least clue to it?"

McCarren stood still, his hands in his pockets, his head cocked up in contemplation of the barred windows. Then he turned his bright hard gaze on his companion.

"That was the queer part of it. I've never spoken of it—but I DID get a clue."

"By Jove! That's interesting. What was it?"

McCarren formed his red lips into a whistle. "Why—that it wasn't a delusion."

He produced his effect—the other turned on him with a pallid stare.

"He murdered the man all right. I tumbled on the truth by the merest accident, when I'd pretty nearly chucked the whole job."

"He murdered him—murdered his cousin?"

"Sure as you live. Only don't split on me. It's about the

queerest business I ever ran into... DO ABOUT IT? Why, what was I to do? I couldn't hang the poor devil, could I? Lord, but I was glad when they collared him, and had him stowed away safe in there!"

The tall man listened with a grave face, grasping Granice's statement in his hand.

"Here—take this; it makes me sick," he said abruptly, thrusting the paper at the reporter; and the two men turned and walked in silence to the gates.

The End

THE DILETTANTE

As first published in Harper's Monthly, December 1903

It was on an impulse hardly needing the arguments he found himself advancing in its favor, that Thursdale, on his way to the club, turned as usual into Mrs. Vervain's street.

The "as usual" was his own qualification of the act; a convenient way of bridging the interval—in days and other sequences—that lay between this visit and the last. It was characteristic of him that he instinctively excluded his call two days earlier, with Ruth Gaynor, from the list of his visits to Mrs. Vervain: the special conditions attending it had made it no more like a visit to Mrs. Vervain than an engraved dinner invitation is like a personal letter. Yet it was to talk over his call with Miss Gaynor that he was now returning to the scene of that episode; and it was because Mrs. Vervain could be trusted to handle the talking over as skilfully as the interview itself that, at her corner, he had felt the dilettante's irresistible craving to take a last look at a work of art that was passing out of his possession.

On the whole, he knew no one better fitted to deal with the unexpected than Mrs. Vervain. She excelled in the rare art of taking things for granted, and Thursdale felt a pardonable pride in the thought that she owed her excellence to his training. Early in his career Thursdale had made the mistake, at the outset of his acquaintance with a lady, of telling her that he loved her and exacting the same avowal in return. The latter part of that episode had been like the long walk back from a picnic, when one has to carry all the crockery one has finished using: it was the last time Thursdale ever allowed himself to be encumbered with the debris of a feast. He thus incidentally learned that the privilege of loving her is one of the least favors that a charming woman can accord; and in seeking to avoid the pitfalls of sentiment he had developed a science of evasion in which the woman of the moment became a mere implement of the game. He owed a great deal of delicate enjoyment to the cultivation of this art. The perils from which it had been his refuge became naively harmless: was it possible that he who now took his easy way along the levels had once preferred to gasp on the raw heights of emotion? Youth is a high-colored season; but he had the satisfaction of feeling that he had entered earlier than most into that chiar'oscuro of sensation where every half-tone has its value.

As a promoter of this pleasure no one he had known was comparable to Mrs. Vervain. He had taught a good many women not to betray their feelings, but he had never before had such fine material to work in. She had been surprisingly crude when he first knew her; capable of making the most awkward inferences, of plunging through thin ice, of recklessly undressing her emotions; but she had acquired, under the discipline of his reticences and evasions, a skill almost equal to his own, and perhaps more remarkable in that it involved keeping time with any tune he played and reading at sight some uncommonly difficult passages.

It had taken Thursdale seven years to form this fine talent; but the result justified the effort. At the crucial moment she had been perfect: her way of greeting Miss Gaynor had made him regret that he had announced his engagement by letter. It was an evasion that confessed a difficulty; a deviation implying an obstacle, where, by common consent, it was agreed to see none; it betrayed, in short, a lack of confidence in the completeness of his method. It had been his pride never to put himself in a position which had to be quitted, as it were, by the back door; but here, as he perceived, the main portals would have opened for him of their own accord. All this, and much more, he read in the finished naturalness with which Mrs. Vervain had met Miss Gaynor. He had never seen a better piece of work: there was no over-eagerness, no suspicious warmth, above all (and this gave her art the grace of a natural quality) there were none of those damnable implications whereby a woman, in welcoming her friend's betrothed, may keep him on pins and needles while she laps the lady in complacency. So masterly a performance, indeed, hardly needed the offset of Miss Gaynor's door-step words—"To be so kind to me, how she must have liked

you!"—though he caught himself wishing it lay within the
bounds of fitness to transmit them, as a final tribute, to the
one woman he knew who was unfailingly certain to enjoy
a good thing. It was perhaps the one drawback to his new
situation that it might develop good things which it would
be impossible to hand on to Margaret Vervain.

The fact that he had made the mistake of underrating his
friend's powers, the consciousness that his writing must have
betrayed his distrust of her efficiency, seemed an added reason
for turning down her street instead of going on to the club.
He would show her that he knew how to value her; he would
ask her to achieve with him a feat infinitely rarer and more
delicate than the one he had appeared to avoid. Incidentally,
he would also dispose of the interval of time before dinner:
ever since he had seen Miss Gaynor off, an hour earlier, on
her return journey to Buffalo, he had been wondering how
he should put in the rest of the afternoon. It was absurd,
how he missed the girl.... Yes, that was it; the desire to talk
about her was, after all, at the bottom of his impulse to
call on Mrs. Vervain! It was absurd, if you like—but it was
delightfully rejuvenating. He could recall the time when
he had been afraid of being obvious: now he felt that this
return to the primitive emotions might be as restorative as a
holiday in the Canadian woods. And it was precisely by the
girl's candor, her directness, her lack of complications, that
he was taken. The sense that she might say something rash at

any moment was positively exhilarating: if she had thrown her arms about him at the station he would not have given a thought to his crumpled dignity. It surprised Thursdale to find what freshness of heart he brought to the adventure; and though his sense of irony prevented his ascribing his intactness to any conscious purpose, he could but rejoice in the fact that his sentimental economies had left him such a large surplus to draw upon.

Mrs. Vervain was at home—as usual. When one visits the cemetery one expects to find the angel on the tombstone, and it struck Thursdale as another proof of his friend's good taste that she had been in no undue haste to change her habits. The whole house appeared to count on his coming; the footman took his hat and overcoat as naturally as though there had been no lapse in his visits; and the drawing-room at once enveloped him in that atmosphere of tacit intelligence which Mrs. Vervain imparted to her very furniture.

It was a surprise that, in this general harmony of circumstances, Mrs. Vervain should herself sound the first false note.

"You?" she exclaimed; and the book she held slipped from her hand.

It was crude, certainly; unless it were a touch of the finest art. The difficulty of classifying it disturbed Thursdale's balance.

"Why not?" he said, restoring the book. "Isn't it my hour?"

And as she made no answer, he added gently, "Unless it's some one else's?"

She laid the book aside and sank back into her chair. "Mine, merely," she said.

"I hope that doesn't mean that you're unwilling to share it?"

"With you? By no means. You're welcome to my last crust."

He looked at her reproachfully. "Do you call this the last?"

She smiled as he dropped into the seat across the hearth. "It's a way of giving it more flavor!"

He returned the smile. "A visit to you doesn't need such condiments."

She took this with just the right measure of retrospective amusement.

"Ah, but I want to put into this one a very special taste," she confessed.

Her smile was so confident, so reassuring, that it lulled him into the imprudence of saying, "Why should you want it to be different from what was always so perfectly right?"

She hesitated. "Doesn't the fact that it's the last constitute a difference?"

"The last—my last visit to you?"

"Oh, metaphorically, I mean—there's a break in the continuity."

Decidedly, she was pressing too hard: unlearning his arts already!

"I don't recognize it," he said. "Unless you make me—" he added, with a note that slightly stirred her attitude of languid attention.

She turned to him with grave eyes. "You recognize no difference whatever?"

"None—except an added link in the chain."

"An added link?"

"In having one more thing to like you for—your letting Miss Gaynor see why I had already so many." He flattered himself that this turn had taken the least hint of fatuity from the phrase.

Mrs. Vervain sank into her former easy pose. "Was it that you came for?" she asked, almost gaily.

"If it is necessary to have a reason—that was one."

"To talk to me about Miss Gaynor?"

"To tell you how she talks about you."

"That will be very interesting—especially if you have seen her since her second visit to me."

"Her second visit?" Thursdale pushed his chair back with a start and moved to another. "She came to see you again?"

"This morning, yes—by appointment."

He continued to look at her blankly. "You sent for her?"

"I didn't have to—she wrote and asked me last night. But no doubt you have seen her since."

Thursdale sat silent. He was trying to separate his words from his thoughts, but they still clung together inextricably. "I saw her off just now at the station."

"And she didn't tell you that she had been here again?"

"There was hardly time, I suppose—there were people about—" he floundered.

"Ah, she'll write, then."

He regained his composure. "Of course she'll write: very often, I hope. You know I'm absurdly in love," he cried audaciously.

She tilted her head back, looking up at him as he leaned against the chimney-piece. He had leaned there so often that the attitude touched a pulse which set up a throbbing in her throat. "Oh, my poor Thursdale!" she murmured.

"I suppose it's rather ridiculous," he owned; and as she remained silent, he added, with a sudden break—"Or have you another reason for pitying me?"

Her answer was another question. "Have you been back to your rooms since you left her?"

"Since I left her at the station? I came straight here."

"Ah, yes—you COULD: there was no reason—" Her words passed into a silent musing.

Thursdale moved nervously nearer. "You said you had something to tell me?"

"Perhaps I had better let her do so. There may be a letter at your rooms."

"A letter? What do you mean? A letter from HER? What has happened?"

His paleness shook her, and she raised a hand of reassurance. "Nothing has happened—perhaps that is just the worst of it. You always HATED, you know," she added incoherently, "to have things happen: you never would let them."

"And now—?"

"Well, that was what she came here for: I supposed you had guessed. To know if anything had happened."

"Had happened?" He gazed at her slowly. "Between you and me?" he said with a rush of light.

The words were so much cruder than any that had ever passed between them that the color rose to her face; but she held his startled gaze.

"You know girls are not quite as unsophisticated as they used to be. Are you surprised that such an idea should occur to her?"

His own color answered hers: it was the only reply that came to him.

Mrs. Vervain went on, smoothly: "I supposed it might have struck you that there were times when we presented that appearance."

He made an impatient gesture. "A man's past is his own!"

"Perhaps—it certainly never belongs to the woman who has shared it. But one learns such truths only by experience; and Miss Gaynor is naturally inexperienced."

"Of course—but—supposing her act a natural one—" he floundered lamentably among his innuendoes—"I still don't see—how there was anything—"

"Anything to take hold of? There wasn't—"

"Well, then—?" escaped him, in crude satisfaction; but as she did not complete the sentence he went on with a faltering laugh: "She can hardly object to the existence of a mere friendship between us!"

"But she does," said Mrs. Vervain.

Thursdale stood perplexed. He had seen, on the previous day, no trace of jealousy or resentment in his betrothed: he could still hear the candid ring of the girl's praise of Mrs. Vervain. If she were such an abyss of insincerity as to dissemble distrust under such frankness, she must at least be more subtle than to bring her doubts to her rival for solution. The situation seemed one through which one could no longer move in a penumbra, and he let in a burst of light with the direct query: "Won't you explain what you mean?"

Mrs. Vervain sat silent, not provokingly, as though to prolong his distress, but as if, in the attenuated phraseology he had taught her, it was difficult to find words robust enough to meet his challenge. It was the first time he had ever asked her to explain anything; and she had lived so long in dread of offering elucidations which were not wanted, that she seemed unable to produce one on the spot.

At last she said slowly: "She came to find out if you were

really free."

Thursdale colored again. "Free?" he stammered, with a sense of physical disgust at contact with such crassness.

"Yes—if I had quite done with you." She smiled in recovered security. "It seems she likes clear outlines; she has a passion for definitions."

"Yes—well?" he said, wincing at the echo of his own subtlety.

"Well—and when I told her that you had never belonged to me, she wanted me to define MY status—to know exactly where I had stood all along."

Thursdale sat gazing at her intently; his hand was not yet on the clue. "And even when you had told her that—"

"Even when I had told her that I had HAD no status—that I had never stood anywhere, in any sense she meant," said Mrs. Vervain, slowly—"even then she wasn't satisfied, it seems."

He uttered an uneasy exclamation. "She didn't believe you, you mean?"

"I mean that she DID believe me: too thoroughly."

"Well, then—in God's name, what did she want?"

"Something more—those were the words she used."

"Something more? Between—between you and me? Is it a conundrum?" He laughed awkwardly.

"Girls are not what they were in my day; they are no longer forbidden to contemplate the relation of the sexes."

"So it seems!" he commented. "But since, in this case, there wasn't any—" he broke off, catching the dawn of a revelation in her gaze.

"That's just it. The unpardonable offence has been—in our not offending."

He flung himself down despairingly. "I give it up!—What did you tell her?" he burst out with sudden crudeness.

"The exact truth. If I had only known," she broke off with a beseeching tenderness, "won't you believe that I would still have lied for you?"

"Lied for me? Why on earth should you have lied for either of us?"

"To save you—to hide you from her to the last! As I've hidden you from myself all these years!" She stood up with a sudden tragic import in her movement. "You believe me capable of that, don't you? If I had only guessed—but I have never known a girl like her; she had the truth out of me with a spring."

"The truth that you and I had never—"

"Had never—never in all these years! Oh, she knew why— she measured us both in a flash. She didn't suspect me of having haggled with you—her words pelted me like hail. 'He just took what he wanted—sifted and sorted you to suit his taste. Burnt out the gold and left a heap of cinders. And you let him—you let yourself be cut in bits'—she mixed her metaphors a little—'be cut in bits, and used or discarded, while all the while every drop of blood in you belonged to him! But he's Shylock—and you have bled to death of the pound of flesh he has cut out of you.' But she despises me the most, you know—far the most—" Mrs. Vervain ended.

The words fell strangely on the scented stillness of the room: they seemed out of harmony with its setting of afternoon intimacy, the kind of intimacy on which at any moment, a visitor might intrude without perceptibly lowering the atmosphere. It was as though a grand opera-singer had strained the acoustics of a private music-room.

Thursdale stood up, facing his hostess. Half the room was between them, but they seemed to stare close at each other now that the veils of reticence and ambiguity had fallen.

His first words were characteristic. "She DOES despise me, then?" he exclaimed.

"She thinks the pound of flesh you took was a little too near the heart."

He was excessively pale. "Please tell me exactly what she said of me."

"She did not speak much of you: she is proud. But I gather that while she understands love or indifference, her eyes have never been opened to the many intermediate shades of feeling. At any rate, she expressed an unwillingness to be taken with reservations—she thinks you would have loved her better if you had loved some one else first. The point of view is original—she insists on a man with a past!"

"Oh, a past—if she's serious—I could rake up a past!" he said with a laugh.

"So I suggested: but she has her eyes on his particular portion of it. She insists on making it a test case. She wanted to know what you had done to me; and before I could guess her drift I blundered into telling her."

Thursdale drew a difficult breath. "I never supposed—your revenge is complete," he said slowly.

He heard a little gasp in her throat. "My revenge? When I sent for you to warn you—to save you from being surprised as I was surprised?"

"You're very good—but it's rather late to talk of saving me." He held out his hand in the mechanical gesture of leave-taking.

"How you must care!—for I never saw you so dull," was her answer. "Don't you see that it's not too late for me to help you?" And as he continued to stare, she brought out sublimely: "Take the rest—in imagination! Let it at least be of that much use to you. Tell her I lied to her—she's too ready to believe it! And so, after all, in a sense, I sha'n't have been wasted."

His stare hung on her, widening to a kind of wonder. She gave the look back brightly, unblushingly, as though the expedient were too simple to need oblique approaches. It was extraordinary how a few words had swept them from an atmosphere of the most complex dissimulations to this contact of naked souls.

It was not in Thursdale to expand with the pressure of fate; but something in him cracked with it, and the rift let in new light. He went up to his friend and took her hand.

"You would do it—you would do it!"

She looked at him, smiling, but her hand shook.

"Good-by," he said, kissing it.

"Good-by? You are going—?"

"To get my letter."

"Your letter? The letter won't matter, if you will only do what I ask."

He returned her gaze. "I might, I suppose, without being out of character. Only, don't you see that if your plan helped me it could only harm her?"

"Harm HER?"

"To sacrifice you wouldn't make me different. I shall go on being what I have always been—sifting and sorting, as she calls it. Do you want my punishment to fall on HER?"

She looked at him long and deeply. "Ah, if I had to choose between you—!"

"You would let her take her chance? But I can't, you see. I must take my punishment alone."

She drew her hand away, sighing. "Oh, there will be no punishment for either of you."

"For either of us? There will be the reading of her letter for me."

She shook her head with a slight laugh. "There will be no letter."

Thursdale faced about from the threshold with fresh life in his look. "No letter? You don't mean—"

"I mean that she's been with you since I saw her—she's seen you and heard your voice. If there IS a letter, she has recalled it—from the first station, by telegraph."

He turned back to the door, forcing an answer to her smile. "But in the mean while I shall have read it," he said.

The door closed on him, and she hid her eyes from the dreadful emptiness of the room.

THE END

THE HOUSE OF THE DEAD HAND

As first published in Atlantic Monthly, August 1904

CHAPTER I

"Above all," the letter ended, "don't leave Siena without seeing Doctor Lombard's Leonardo. Lombard is a queer old Englishman, a mystic or a madman (if the two are not synonymous), and a devout student of the Italian Renaissance. He has lived for years in Italy, exploring its remotest corners, and has lately picked up an undoubted Leonardo, which came to light in a farmhouse near Bergamo. It is believed to be one of the missing pictures mentioned by Vasari, and is at any rate, according to the most competent authorities, a genuine and almost untouched example of the best period.

"Lombard is a queer stick, and jealous of showing his treasures; but we struck up a friendship when I was working on the Sodomas in Siena three years ago, and if you will give him the enclosed line you may get a peep at the Leonardo. Probably not more than a peep, though, for I hear he refuses to have it reproduced. I want badly to use it in my monograph on the Windsor drawings, so please see what you can do for me, and if you can't persuade him to let you take a photograph or make a sketch, at least jot down a detailed description of the picture and get from him all the facts you can. I hear that the French and Italian governments have offered him a large advance on his purchase, but that he refuses to sell at any price, though he certainly can't afford such luxuries; in fact, I don't see where he got enough money to buy the picture. He lives in the Via Papa Giulio."

Wyant sat at the table d'hote of his hotel, re-reading his friend's letter over a late luncheon. He had been five days in Siena without having found time to call on Doctor Lombard; not from any indifference to the opportunity presented, but because it was his first visit to the strange red city and he was still under the spell of its more conspicuous wonders—the brick palaces flinging out their wrought-iron torch-holders with a gesture of arrogant suzerainty; the great council-chamber emblazoned with civic allegories; the pageant of Pope Julius on the Library walls; the Sodomas smiling balefully through the dusk of mouldering chapels—and it was only when his first hunger was appeased that he remembered that one course in the banquet was still untasted.

He put the letter in his pocket and turned to leave the room, with a nod to its only other occupant, an olive-skinned young man with lustrous eyes and a low collar, who sat on the other side of the table, perusing the Fanfulla di Domenica. This gentleman, his daily vis-a-vis, returned the nod with a Latin eloquence of gesture, and Wyant passed on to the ante-chamber, where he paused to light a cigarette. He was just restoring the case to his pocket when he heard a hurried step behind him, and the lustrous-eyed young man advanced through the glass doors of the dining-room.

"Pardon me, sir," he said in measured English, and with an intonation of exquisite politeness; "you have let this letter fall."

Wyant, recognizing his friend's note of introduction to Doctor Lombard, took it with a word of thanks, and was about to turn away when he perceived that the eyes of his fellow diner remained fixed on him with a gaze of melancholy interrogation.

"Again pardon me," the young man at length ventured, "but are you by chance the friend of the illustrious Doctor Lombard?"

"No," returned Wyant, with the instinctive Anglo-Saxon distrust of foreign advances. Then, fearing to appear rude, he said with a guarded politeness: "Perhaps, by the way, you can tell me the number of his house. I see it is not given here."

The young man brightened perceptibly. "The number of the house is thirteen; but any one can indicate it to you—it is well known in Siena. It is called," he continued after a moment, "the House of the Dead Hand."

Wyant stared. "What a queer name!" he said.

"The name comes from an antique hand of marble which for many hundred years has been above the door."

Wyant was turning away with a gesture of thanks, when the other added: "If you would have the kindness to ring twice."

"To ring twice?"

"At the doctor's." The young man smiled. "It is the custom."

It was a dazzling March afternoon, with a shower of sun from the mid-blue, and a marshalling of slaty clouds behind the umber-colored hills. For nearly an hour Wyant loitered on the Lizza, watching the shadows race across the naked landscape and the thunder blacken in the west; then he decided to set out for the House of the Dead Hand. The map in his guidebook showed him that the Via Papa Giulio was one of the streets which radiate from the Piazza, and thither he bent his course, pausing at every other step to fill his eye with some fresh image of weather-beaten beauty. The clouds had rolled upward, obscuring the sunshine and hanging like a funereal baldachin above the projecting cornices of Doctor Lombard's street, and Wyant walked for some distance in the shade of the beetling palace fronts before his eye fell on a doorway surmounted by a sallow marble hand. He stood for a moment staring up at the strange emblem. The hand was a woman's—a dead drooping hand, which hung there convulsed and helpless, as though it had been thrust forth in denunciation of some evil mystery within the house, and had sunk struggling into death.

A girl who was drawing water from the well in the court said that the English doctor lived on the first floor, and Wyant, passing through a glazed door, mounted the damp degrees of a vaulted stairway with a plaster AEsculapius mouldering in a niche on the landing. Facing the AEsculapius was another door, and as Wyant put his hand on the bell-rope he remembered his unknown friend's injunction, and rang twice.

His ring was answered by a peasant woman with a low forehead and small close-set eyes, who, after a prolonged scrutiny of himself, his card, and his letter of introduction, left him standing in a high, cold ante-chamber floored with brick. He heard her wooden pattens click down an interminable corridor, and after some delay she returned and told him to follow her.

They passed through a long saloon, bare as the ante-chamber, but loftily vaulted, and frescoed with a seventeenth-century Triumph of Scipio or Alexander—martial figures following Wyant with the filmed melancholy gaze of shades in limbo. At the end of this apartment he was admitted to a smaller room, with the same atmosphere of mortal cold, but showing more obvious signs of occupancy. The walls were covered with tapestry which had faded to the gray-brown tints of decaying vegetation, so that the young man felt as though he were entering a sunless autumn wood. Against these hangings stood a few tall cabinets on heavy gilt feet, and at a table in the window three persons were seated: an elderly lady who was warming her hands over a brazier, a girl bent above a strip of needle-work, and an old man.

As the latter advanced toward Wyant, the young man was conscious of staring with unseemly intentness at his small round-backed figure, dressed with shabby disorder and surmounted by a wonderful head, lean, vulpine, eagle-beaked as that of some art-loving despot of the Renaissance: a head combining the venerable hair and large prominent eyes of the humanist with the greedy profile of the adventurer. Wyant, in musing on the Italian portrait-medals of the fifteenth century, had often fancied that only in that period of fierce individualism could types so paradoxical have been produced; yet the subtle craftsmen who committed them to the bronze had never drawn a face more strangely stamped with contradictory passions than that of Doctor Lombard.

"I am glad to see you," he said to Wyant, extending a hand which seemed a mere framework held together by knotted veins. "We lead a quiet life here and receive few visitors, but any friend of Professor Clyde's is welcome." Then, with a gesture which included the two women, he added dryly: "My wife and daughter often talk of Professor Clyde."

"Oh yes—he used to make me such nice toast; they don't understand toast in Italy," said Mrs. Lombard in a high plaintive voice.

It would have been difficult, from Doctor Lombard's

manner and appearance to guess his nationality; but his wife was so inconsciently and ineradicably English that even the silhouette of her cap seemed a protest against Continental laxities. She was a stout fair woman, with pale cheeks netted with red lines. A brooch with a miniature portrait sustained a bogwood watch-chain upon her bosom, and at her elbow lay a heap of knitting and an old copy of The Queen.

The young girl, who had remained standing, was a slim replica of her mother, with an apple-cheeked face and opaque blue eyes. Her small head was prodigally laden with braids of dull fair hair, and she might have had a kind of transient prettiness but for the sullen droop of her round mouth. It was hard to say whether her expression implied ill-temper or apathy; but Wyant was struck by the contrast between the fierce vitality of the doctor's age and the inanimateness of his daughter's youth.

Seating himself in the chair which his host advanced, the young man tried to open the conversation by addressing to Mrs. Lombard some random remark on the beauties of Siena. The lady murmured a resigned assent, and Doctor Lombard interposed with a smile: "My dear sir, my wife considers Siena a most salubrious spot, and is favorably impressed by the cheapness of the marketing; but she deplores the total absence of muffins and cannel coal, and cannot resign herself to the Italian method of dusting furniture."

"But they don't, you know—they don't dust it!" Mrs.

Lombard protested, without showing any resentment of her husband's manner.

"Precisely—they don't dust it. Since we have lived in Siena we have not once seen the cobwebs removed from the battlements of the Mangia. Can you conceive of such housekeeping? My wife has never yet dared to write it home to her aunts at Bonchurch."

Mrs. Lombard accepted in silence this remarkable statement of her views, and her husband, with a malicious smile at Wyant's embarrassment, planted himself suddenly before the young man.

"And now," said he, "do you want to see my Leonardo?"

"DO I?" cried Wyant, on his feet in a flash.

The doctor chuckled. "Ah," he said, with a kind of crooning deliberation, "that's the way they all behave—that's what they all come for." He turned to his daughter with another variation of mockery in his smile. "Don't fancy it's for your beaux yeux, my dear; or for the mature charms of Mrs. Lombard," he added, glaring suddenly at his wife, who had taken up her knitting and was softly murmuring over the number of her stitches.

Neither lady appeared to notice his pleasantries, and he continued, addressing himself to Wyant: "They all come—they all come; but many are called and few are chosen." His voice sank to solemnity. "While I live," he said, "no unworthy eye shall desecrate that picture. But I will not do my friend Clyde the injustice to suppose that he would send an unworthy representative. He tells me he wishes a description of the picture for his book; and you shall describe it to him—if you can."

Wyant hesitated, not knowing whether it was a propitious moment to put in his appeal for a photograph.

"Well, sir," he said, "you know Clyde wants me to take away all I can of it."

Doctor Lombard eyed him sardonically. "You're welcome to take away all you can carry," he replied; adding, as he turned to his daughter: "That is, if he has your permission, Sybilla."

The girl rose without a word, and laying aside her work, took a key from a secret drawer in one of the cabinets, while the doctor continued in the same note of grim jocularity: "For you must know that the picture is not mine—it is my daughter's."

He followed with evident amusement the surprised glance which Wyant turned on the young girl's impassive figure.

"Sybilla," he pursued, "is a votary of the arts; she has inherited her fond father's passion for the unattainable. Luckily, however, she also recently inherited a tidy legacy from her grandmother; and having seen the Leonardo, on which its discoverer had placed a price far beyond my reach, she took a step which deserves to go down to history: she invested her whole inheritance in the purchase of the picture, thus enabling me to spend my closing years in communion with one of the world's masterpieces. My dear sir, could Antigone do more?"

The object of this strange eulogy had meanwhile drawn aside one of the tapestry hangings, and fitted her key into a concealed door.

"Come," said Doctor Lombard, "let us go before the light fails us."

Wyant glanced at Mrs. Lombard, who continued to knit impassively.

"No, no," said his host, "my wife will not come with us. You might not suspect it from her conversation, but my wife has no feeling for art—Italian art, that is; for no one is fonder of our early Victorian school."

"Frith's Railway Station, you know," said Mrs. Lombard, smiling. "I like an animated picture."

Miss Lombard, who had unlocked the door, held back the tapestry to let her father and Wyant pass out; then she followed them down a narrow stone passage with another door at its end. This door was iron-barred, and Wyant noticed that it had a complicated patent lock. The girl fitted another key into the lock, and Doctor Lombard led the way into a small room. The dark panelling of this apartment was irradiated by streams of yellow light slanting through the disbanded thunder clouds, and in the central brightness hung a picture concealed by a curtain of faded velvet.

"A little too bright, Sybilla," said Doctor Lombard. His face had grown solemn, and his mouth twitched nervously as his daughter drew a linen drapery across the upper part of the window.

"That will do—that will do." He turned impressively to Wyant. "Do you see the pomegranate bud in this rug? Place yourself there—keep your left foot on it, please. And now, Sybilla, draw the cord."

Miss Lombard advanced and placed her hand on a cord hidden behind the velvet curtain.

"Ah," said the doctor, "one moment: I should like you, while looking at the picture, to have in mind a few lines of verse. Sybilla—"

Without the slightest change of countenance, and with a promptness which proved her to be prepared for the request, Miss Lombard began to recite, in a full round voice like her mother's, St. Bernard's invocation to the Virgin, in the thirty-third canto of the Paradise.

"Thank you, my dear," said her father, drawing a deep breath as she ended. "That unapproachable combination of vowel sounds prepares one better than anything I know for the contemplation of the picture."

As he spoke the folds of velvet slowly parted, and the Leonardo appeared in its frame of tarnished gold:

From the nature of Miss Lombard's recitation Wyant had expected a sacred subject, and his surprise was therefore great

154

as the composition was gradually revealed by the widening division of the curtain.

In the background a steel-colored river wound through a pale calcareous landscape; while to the left, on a lonely peak, a crucified Christ hung livid against indigo clouds. The central figure of the foreground, however, was that of a woman seated in an antique chair of marble with bas-reliefs of dancing maenads. Her feet rested on a meadow sprinkled with minute wild-flowers, and her attitude of smiling majesty recalled that of Dosso Dossi's Circe. She wore a red robe, flowing in closely fluted lines from under a fancifully embroidered cloak. Above her high forehead the crinkled golden hair flowed sideways beneath a veil; one hand drooped on the arm of her chair; the other held up an inverted human skull, into which a young Dionysus, smooth, brown and sidelong as the St. John of the Louvre, poured a stream of wine from a high-poised flagon. At the lady's feet lay the symbols of art and luxury: a flute and a roll of music, a platter heaped with grapes and roses, the torso of a Greek statuette, and a bowl overflowing with coins and jewels; behind her, on the chalky hilltop, hung the crucified Christ. A scroll in a corner of the foreground bore the legend: Lux Mundi.

Wyant, emerging from the first plunge of wonder, turned inquiringly toward his companions. Neither had moved. Miss Lombard stood with her hand on the cord, her lids lowered, her mouth drooping; the doctor, his strange Thoth-like profile turned toward his guest, was still lost in rapt contemplation of his treasure.

Wyant addressed the young girl.

"You are fortunate," he said, "to be the possessor of anything so perfect."

"It is considered very beautiful," she said coldly.

"Beautiful—BEAUTIFUL!" the doctor burst out. "Ah, the poor, worn out, over-worked word! There are no adjectives in the language fresh enough to describe such pristine brilliancy; all their brightness has been worn off by misuse. Think of the things that have been called beautiful, and then look at THAT!"

"It is worthy of a new vocabulary," Wyant agreed.

"Yes," Doctor Lombard continued, "my daughter is indeed fortunate. She has chosen what Catholics call the higher life—the counsel of perfection. What other private person enjoys the same opportunity of understanding the master? Who else lives under the same roof with an untouched masterpiece of Leonardo's? Think of the happiness of being always under the influence of such a creation; of living INTO it; of partaking of it in daily and hourly communion! This room is a chapel; the sight of that picture is a sacrament. What an atmosphere for a young life to unfold itself in! My daughter is singularly blessed. Sybilla, point out some of the details to Mr. Wyant; I see that he will appreciate them."

The girl turned her dense blue eyes toward Wyant; then, glancing away from him, she pointed to the canvas.

"Notice the modeling of the left hand," she began in a monotonous voice; "it recalls the hand of the Mona Lisa. The head of the naked genius will remind you of that of the St. John of the Louvre, but it is more purely pagan and is turned a little less to the right. The embroidery on the cloak is symbolic: you will see that the roots of this plant have burst through the vase. This recalls the famous definition of Hamlet's character in Wilhelm Meister. Here are the mystic rose, the flame, and the serpent, emblem of eternity. Some of the other symbols we have not yet been able to decipher."

Wyant watched her curiously; she seemed to be reciting a lesson.

"And the picture itself?" he said. "How do you explain that? Lux Mundi—what a curious device to connect with such a subject! What can it mean?"

Miss Lombard dropped her eyes: the answer was evidently not included in her lesson.

"What, indeed?" the doctor interposed. "What does life mean? As one may define it in a hundred different ways, so one may find a hundred different meanings in this picture. Its symbolism is as many-faceted as a well-cut diamond. Who, for instance, is that divine lady? Is it she who is the true Lux Mundi—the light reflected from jewels and young eyes, from polished marble and clear waters and statues of

157

bronze? Or is that the Light of the World, extinguished on yonder stormy hill, and is this lady the Pride of Life, feasting blindly on the wine of iniquity, with her back turned to the light which has shone for her in vain? Something of both these meanings may be traced in the picture; but to me it symbolizes rather the central truth of existence: that all that is raised in incorruption is sown in corruption; art, beauty, love, religion; that all our wine is drunk out of skulls, and poured for us by the mysterious genius of a remote and cruel past."

The doctor's face blazed: his bent figure seemed to straighten itself and become taller.

"Ah," he cried, growing more dithyrambic, "how lightly you ask what it means! How confidently you expect an answer! Yet here am I who have given my life to the study of the Renaissance; who have violated its tomb, laid open its dead body, and traced the course of every muscle, bone, and artery; who have sucked its very soul from the pages of poets and humanists; who have wept and believed with Joachim of Flora, smiled and doubted with AEneas Sylvius Piccolomini; who have patiently followed to its source the least inspiration of the masters, and groped in neolithic caverns and Babylonian ruins for the first unfolding tendrils of the arabesques of Mantegna and Crivelli; and I tell you that I stand abashed and ignorant before the mystery of this picture. It means nothing—it means all things. It may represent the period which saw its creation; it may represent all ages past and to come. There are volumes of meaning in the tiniest emblem on the lady's cloak; the blossoms of its border are rooted in the deepest soil of myth and tradition. Don't ask what it means, young man, but bow your head in thankfulness for having seen it!"

Miss Lombard laid her hand on his arm.

"Don't excite yourself, father," she said in the detached tone of a professional nurse.

He answered with a despairing gesture. "Ah, it's easy for you to talk. You have years and years to spend with it; I am an old man, and every moment counts!"

"It's bad for you," she repeated with gentle obstinacy.

The doctor's sacred fury had in fact burnt itself out. He dropped into a seat with dull eyes and slackening lips, and his daughter drew the curtain across the picture.

Wyant turned away reluctantly. He felt that his opportunity was slipping from him, yet he dared not refer to Clyde's wish for a photograph. He now understood the meaning of the laugh with which Doctor Lombard had given him leave to carry away all the details he could remember. The picture was so dazzling, so unexpected, so crossed with elusive and contradictory suggestions, that the most alert observer, when placed suddenly before it, must lose his coordinating faculty in a sense of confused wonder. Yet how valuable to Clyde the record of such a work would be! In some ways it seemed to be the summing up of the master's thought, the key to his enigmatic philosophy.

The doctor had risen and was walking slowly toward the door. His daughter unlocked it, and Wyant followed them back in silence to the room in which they had left Mrs. Lombard. That lady was no longer there, and he could think of no excuse for lingering.

He thanked the doctor, and turned to Miss Lombard, who stood in the middle of the room as though awaiting farther orders.

"It is very good of you," he said, "to allow one even a glimpse of such a treasure."

She looked at him with her odd directness. "You will come again?" she said quickly; and turning to her father she added: "You know what Professor Clyde asked. This gentleman cannot give him any account of the picture without seeing it again."

Doctor Lombard glanced at her vaguely; he was still like a person in a trance.

"Eh?" he said, rousing himself with an effort.

"I said, father, that Mr. Wyant must see the picture again if he is to tell Professor Clyde about it," Miss Lombard repeated with extraordinary precision of tone.

Wyant was silent. He had the puzzled sense that his wishes were being divined and gratified for reasons with which he was in no way connected.

"Well, well," the doctor muttered, "I don't say no—I don't say no. I know what Clyde wants—I don't refuse to help him." He turned to Wyant. "You may come again—you may make notes," he added with a sudden effort. "Jot down what occurs to you. I'm willing to concede that."

Wyant again caught the girl's eye, but its emphatic message perplexed him.

"You're very good," he said tentatively, "but the fact is the picture is so mysterious—so full of complicated detail—that I'm afraid no notes I could make would serve Clyde's purpose as well as—as a photograph, say. If you would allow me—"

Miss Lombard's brow darkened, and her father raised his head furiously.

"A photograph? A photograph, did you say? Good God, man, not ten people have been allowed to set foot in that room! A PHOTOGRAPH?"

Wyant saw his mistake, but saw also that he had gone too far to retreat.

"I know, sir, from what Clyde has told me, that you object to having any reproduction of the picture published; but he hoped you might let me take a photograph for his personal use—not to be reproduced in his book, but simply to give him something to work by. I should take the photograph myself, and the negative would of course be yours. If you wished it, only one impression would be struck off, and that one Clyde could return to you when he had done with it."

Doctor Lombard interrupted him with a snarl. "When he had done with it? Just so: I thank thee for that word! When it had been re-photographed, drawn, traced, autotyped, passed about from hand to hand, defiled by every ignorant eye in England, vulgarized by the blundering praise of every art-scribbler in Europe! Bah! I'd as soon give you the picture itself: why don't you ask for that?"

"Well, sir," said Wyant calmly, "if you will trust me with it, I'll engage to take it safely to England and back, and to let no eye but Clyde's see it while it is out of your keeping."

The doctor received this remarkable proposal in silence; then he burst into a laugh.

"Upon my soul!" he said with sardonic good humor.

It was Miss Lombard's turn to look perplexedly at Wyant. His last words and her father's unexpected reply had evidently carried her beyond her depth.

"Well, sir, am I to take the picture?" Wyant smilingly pursued.

"No, young man; nor a photograph of it. Nor a sketch, either; mind that,—nothing that can be reproduced. Sybilla," he cried with sudden passion, "swear to me that the picture shall never be reproduced! No photograph, no sketch—now or afterward. Do you hear me?"

"Yes, father," said the girl quietly.

"The vandals," he muttered, "the desecrators of beauty; if I thought it would ever get into their hands I'd burn it first, by

God!" He turned to Wyant, speaking more quietly. "I said you might come back—I never retract what I say. But you must give me your word that no one but Clyde shall see the notes you make."

Wyant was growing warm.

"If you won't trust me with a photograph I wonder you trust me not to show my notes!" he exclaimed.

The doctor looked at him with a malicious smile.

"Humph!" he said; "would they be of much use to anybody?"

Wyant saw that he was losing ground and controlled his impatience.

"To Clyde, I hope, at any rate," he answered, holding out his hand. The doctor shook it without a trace of resentment, and Wyant added: "When shall I come, sir?"

"To-morrow—to-morrow morning," cried Miss Lombard, speaking suddenly.

She looked fixedly at her father, and he shrugged his shoulders.

"The picture is hers," he said to Wyant.

In the ante-chamber the young man was met by the woman who had admitted him. She handed him his hat and stick, and turned to unbar the door. As the bolt slipped back he felt a touch on his arm.

"You have a letter?" she said in a low tone.

"A letter?" He stared. "What letter?"

She shrugged her shoulders, and drew back to let him pass.

CHAPTER II

As Wyant emerged from the house he paused once more to glance up at its scarred brick facade. The marble hand drooped tragically above the entrance: in the waning light it seemed to have relaxed into the passiveness of despair, and Wyant stood musing on its hidden meaning. But the Dead Hand was not the only mysterious thing about Doctor Lombard's house. What were the relations between Miss Lombard and her father? Above all, between Miss Lombard and her picture? She did not look like a person capable of a disinterested passion for the arts; and there had been moments when it struck Wyant that she hated the picture.

The sky at the end of the street was flooded with turbulent yellow light, and the young man turned his steps toward the church of San Domenico, in the hope of catching the lingering brightness on Sodoma's St. Catherine.

The great bare aisles were almost dark when he entered, and he had to grope his way to the chapel steps. Under the momentary evocation of the sunset, the saint's figure emerged pale and swooning from the dusk, and the warm light gave a sensual tinge to her ecstasy. The flesh seemed to glow and heave, the eyelids to tremble; Wyant stood fascinated by the accidental collaboration of light and color.

Suddenly he noticed that something white had fluttered to the ground at his feet. He stooped and picked up a small thin sheet of note-paper, folded and sealed like an old-fashioned letter, and bearing the superscription:—

To the Count Ottaviano Celsi.

Wyant stared at this mysterious document. Where had it come from? He was distinctly conscious of having seen it fall through the air, close to his feet. He glanced up at the dark ceiling of the chapel; then he turned and looked about the church. There was only one figure in it, that of a man who knelt near the high altar.

Suddenly Wyant recalled the question of Doctor Lombard's maid-servant. Was this the letter she had asked for? Had he been unconsciously carrying it about with him all the afternoon? Who was Count Ottaviano Celsi, and how came Wyant to have been chosen to act as that nobleman's ambulant letter-box?

Wyant laid his hat and stick on the chapel steps and began to explore his pockets, in the irrational hope of finding there some clue to the mystery; but they held nothing which he had not himself put there, and he was reduced to wondering how the letter, supposing some unknown hand to have bestowed it on him, had happened to fall out while he stood motionless before the picture.

At this point he was disturbed by a step on the floor of the aisle, and turning, he saw his lustrous-eyed neighbor of the table d'hote.

The young man bowed and waved an apologetic hand.

"I do not intrude?" he inquired suavely.

Without waiting for a reply, he mounted the steps of the chapel, glancing about him with the affable air of an afternoon caller.

"I see," he remarked with a smile, "that you know the hour at which our saint should be visited."

Wyant agreed that the hour was indeed felicitous.

The stranger stood beamingly before the picture.

"What grace! What poetry!" he murmured, apostrophizing the St. Catherine, but letting his glance slip rapidly about the chapel as he spoke.

Wyant, detecting the manoeuvre, murmured a brief assent.

"But it is cold here—mortally cold; you do not find it so?" The intruder put on his hat. "It is permitted at this hour—when the church is empty. And you, my dear sir—do you not feel the dampness? You are an artist, are you not? And to artists it is permitted to cover the head when they are engaged in the study of the paintings."

He darted suddenly toward the steps and bent over Wyant's hat.

"Permit me—cover yourself!" he said a moment later, holding out the hat with an ingratiating gesture.

A light flashed on Wyant.

"Perhaps," he said, looking straight at the young man, "you will tell me your name. My own is Wyant."

The stranger, surprised, but not disconcerted, drew forth a coroneted card, which he offered with a low bow. On the card was engraved:—

Il Conte Ottaviano Celsi.

"I am much obliged to you," said Wyant; "and I may as well tell you that the letter which you apparently expected to find in the lining of my hat is not there, but in my pocket."

He drew it out and handed it to its owner, who had grown very pale.

"And now," Wyant continued, "you will perhaps be good enough to tell me what all this means."

There was no mistaking the effect produced on Count Ottaviano by this request. His lips moved, but he achieved only an ineffectual smile.

"I suppose you know," Wyant went on, his anger rising at the sight of the other's discomfiture, "that you have taken an unwarrantable liberty. I don't yet understand what part I have been made to play, but it's evident that you have made use of me to serve some purpose of your own, and I propose to know the reason why."

Count Ottaviano advanced with an imploring gesture.

"Sir," he pleaded, "you permit me to speak?"

"I expect you to," cried Wyant. "But not here," he added, hearing the clank of the verger's keys. "It is growing dark, and we shall be turned out in a few minutes."

He walked across the church, and Count Ottaviano

followed him out into the deserted square.

"Now," said Wyant, pausing on the steps.

The Count, who had regained some measure of self-possession, began to speak in a high key, with an accompaniment of conciliatory gesture.

"My dear sir—my dear Mr. Wyant—you find me in an abominable position—that, as a man of honor, I immediately confess. I have taken advantage of you—yes! I have counted on your amiability, your chivalry—too far, perhaps? I confess it! But what could I do? It was to oblige a lady"—he laid a hand on his heart—"a lady whom I would die to serve!" He went on with increasing volubility, his deliberate English swept away by a torrent of Italian, through which Wyant, with some difficulty, struggled to a comprehension of the case.

Count Ottaviano, according to his own statement, had come to Siena some months previously, on business connected with his mother's property; the paternal estate being near Orvieto, of which ancient city his father was syndic. Soon after his arrival in Siena the young Count had met the incomparable daughter of Doctor Lombard, and falling deeply in love with her, had prevailed on his parents to ask her hand in marriage. Doctor Lombard had not opposed his suit, but when the question of settlements arose it became known that Miss Lombard, who was possessed of a small property in her own right, had a short time before invested the whole amount in the purchase of the Bergamo Leonardo. Thereupon Count Ottaviano's parents had politely suggested that she should sell the picture and thus recover her independence; and this proposal being met by a curt refusal from Doctor Lombard, they had withdrawn their consent to their son's marriage. The young lady's attitude had hitherto been one of passive submission; she was horribly afraid of her father, and would never venture openly to oppose him; but she had made known to Ottaviano her intention of not giving him up, of waiting patiently till events should take a more favorable turn. She seemed hardly aware, the Count said with a sigh, that the means of escape lay in her own hands; that she was of age, and had a right to sell the picture, and to marry without asking her father's consent. Meanwhile her suitor spared no pains to keep himself before her, to remind her that he, too, was waiting and would never give her up.

Doctor Lombard, who suspected the young man of trying to persuade Sybilla to sell the picture, had forbidden the lovers to meet or to correspond; they were thus driven to clandestine communication, and had several times, the Count ingenuously avowed, made use of the doctor's visitors as a means of exchanging letters.

"And you told the visitors to ring twice?" Wyant interposed.

The young man extended his hands in a deprecating

gesture. Could Mr. Wyant blame him? He was young, he was ardent, he was enamored! The young lady had done him the supreme honor of avowing her attachment, of pledging her unalterable fidelity; should he suffer his devotion to be outdone? But his purpose in writing to her, he admitted, was not merely to reiterate his fidelity; he was trying by every means in his power to induce her to sell the picture. He had organized a plan of action; every detail was complete; if she would but have the courage to carry out his instructions he would answer for the result. His idea was that she should secretly retire to a convent of which his aunt was the Mother Superior, and from that stronghold should transact the sale of the Leonardo. He had a purchaser ready, who was willing to pay a large sum; a sum, Count Ottaviano whispered, considerably in excess of the young lady's original inheritance; once the picture sold, it could, if necessary, be removed by force from Doctor Lombard's house, and his daughter, being safely in the convent, would be spared the painful scenes incidental to the removal. Finally, if Doctor Lombard were vindictive enough to refuse his consent to her marriage, she had only to make a sommation respectueuse, and at the end of the prescribed delay no power on earth could prevent her becoming the wife of Count Ottaviano.

Wyant's anger had fallen at the recital of this simple romance. It was absurd to be angry with a young man who confided his secrets to the first stranger he met in the streets, and placed his hand on his heart whenever he mentioned the name of his betrothed. The easiest way out of the business was to take it as a joke. Wyant had played the wall to this new Pyramus and Thisbe, and was philosophic enough to laugh at the part he had unwittingly performed.

He held out his hand with a smile to Count Ottaviano.

"I won't deprive you any longer," he said, "of the pleasure of reading your letter."

"Oh, sir, a thousand thanks! And when you return to the casa Lombard, you will take a message from me—the letter she expected this afternoon?"

"The letter she expected?" Wyant paused. "No, thank you. I thought you understood that where I come from we don't do that kind of thing—knowingly."

"But, sir, to serve a young lady!"

"I'm sorry for the young lady, if what you tell me is true"— the Count's expressive hands resented the doubt—"but remember that if I am under obligations to any one in this matter, it is to her father, who has admitted me to his house and has allowed me to see his picture."

"HIS picture? Hers!"

"Well, the house is his, at all events."

"Unhappily—since to her it is a dungeon!"

"Why doesn't she leave it, then?" exclaimed Wyant impatiently.

The Count clasped his hands. "Ah, how you say that—

with what force, with what virility! If you would but say it to HER in that tone—you, her countryman! She has no one to advise her; the mother is an idiot; the father is terrible; she is in his power; it is my belief that he would kill her if she resisted him. Mr. Wyant, I tremble for her life while she remains in that house!"

"Oh, come," said Wyant lightly, "they seem to understand each other well enough. But in any case, you must see that I can't interfere—at least you would if you were an Englishman," he added with an escape of contempt.

CHAPTER III

Wyant's affiliations in Siena being restricted to an acquaintance with his land-lady, he was forced to apply to her for the verification of Count Ottaviano's story.

The young nobleman had, it appeared, given a perfectly correct account of his situation. His father, Count Celsi-Mongirone, was a man of distinguished family and some wealth. He was syndic of Orvieto, and lived either in that town or on his neighboring estate of Mongirone. His wife owned a large property near Siena, and Count Ottaviano, who was the second son, came there from time to time to look into its management. The eldest son was in the army, the youngest in the Church; and an aunt of Count Ottaviano's was Mother Superior of the Visitandine convent in Siena. At one time it had been said that Count Ottaviano, who was a most amiable and accomplished young man, was to marry the daughter of the strange Englishman, Doctor Lombard, but difficulties having arisen as to the adjustment of the young lady's dower, Count Celsi-Mongirone had very properly broken off the match. It was sad for the young man, however, who was said to be deeply in love, and to find frequent excuses for coming to Siena to inspect his mother's estate.

Viewed in the light of Count Ottaviano's personality the story had a tinge of opera bouffe; but the next morning, as Wyant mounted the stairs of the House of the Dead Hand, the situation insensibly assumed another aspect. It was impossible to take Doctor Lombard lightly; and there was a suggestion of fatality in the appearance of his gaunt dwelling. Who could tell amid what tragic records of domestic tyranny and fluttering broken purposes the little drama of Miss Lombard's fate was being played out? Might not the accumulated influences of such a house modify the lives within it in a manner unguessed by the inmates of a suburban villa with sanitary plumbing and a telephone?

One person, at least, remained unperturbed by such fanciful problems; and that was Mrs. Lombard, who, at Wyant's entrance, raised a placidly wrinkled brow from her knitting. The morning was mild, and her chair had been wheeled into a bar of sunshine near the window, so that she made a cheerful spot of prose in the poetic gloom of her surroundings.

"What a nice morning!" she said; "it must be delightful weather at Bonchurch."

Her dull blue glance wandered across the narrow street with its threatening house fronts, and fluttered back baffled, like a bird with clipped wings. It was evident, poor lady, that she had never seen beyond the opposite houses.

Wyant was not sorry to find her alone. Seeing that she was surprised at his reappearance he said at once: "I have come back to study Miss Lombard's picture."

"Oh, the picture—" Mrs. Lombard's face expressed a gentle disappointment, which might have been boredom in a person of acuter sensibilities. "It's an original Leonardo, you know," she said mechanically.

"And Miss Lombard is very proud of it, I suppose? She seems to have inherited her father's love for art."

Mrs. Lombard counted her stitches, and he went on: "It's unusual in so young a girl. Such tastes generally develop later."

Mrs. Lombard looked up eagerly. "That's what I say! I was quite different at her age, you know. I liked dancing, and doing a pretty bit of fancy-work. Not that I couldn't sketch, too; I had a master down from London. My aunts have some of my crayons hung up in their drawing-room now—I did a view of Kenilworth which was thought pleasing. But I liked a picnic, too, or a pretty walk through the woods with young people of my own age. I say it's more natural, Mr. Wyant; one may have a feeling for art, and do crayons that are worth framing, and yet not give up everything else. I was taught that there were other things."

Wyant, half-ashamed of provoking these innocent confidences, could not resist another question. "And Miss Lombard cares for nothing else?"

Her mother looked troubled.

"Sybilla is so clever—she says I don't understand. You know how self-confident young people are! My husband never said that of me, now—he knows I had an excellent education. My aunts were very particular; I was brought up to have opinions, and my husband has always respected them. He says himself that he wouldn't for the world miss hearing my opinion on any subject; you may have noticed that he often refers to my tastes. He has always respected my preference for living in England; he likes to hear me give my reasons for it. He is so much interested in my ideas that he often says he knows just what I am going to say before I speak. But Sybilla does not care for what I think—"

At this point Doctor Lombard entered. He glanced sharply at Wyant. "The servant is a fool; she didn't tell me you were here." His eye turned to his wife. "Well, my dear, what have you been telling Mr. Wyant? About the aunts at Bonchurch, I'll be bound!"

Mrs. Lombard looked triumphantly at Wyant, and her husband rubbed his hooked fingers, with a smile.

"Mrs. Lombard's aunts are very superior women. They subscribe to the circulating library, and borrow Good Words and the Monthly Packet from the curate's wife across the way. They have the rector to tea twice a year, and keep a page-boy, and are visited by two baronets' wives. They devoted themselves to the education of their orphan niece, and I think I may say without boasting that Mrs. Lombard's conversation shows marked traces of the advantages she enjoyed."

Mrs. Lombard colored with pleasure.

"I was telling Mr. Wyant that my aunts were very particular."

"Quite so, my dear; and did you mention that they never sleep in anything but linen, and that Miss Sophia puts away the furs and blankets every spring with her own hands? Both those facts are interesting to the student of human nature." Doctor Lombard glanced at his watch. "But we are missing an incomparable moment; the light is perfect at this hour."

Wyant rose, and the doctor led him through the tapestried door and down the passageway.

The light was, in fact, perfect, and the picture shone with an inner radiancy, as though a lamp burned behind the soft screen of the lady's flesh. Every detail of the foreground detached itself with jewel-like precision. Wyant noticed a dozen accessories which had escaped him on the previous day.

He drew out his note-book, and the doctor, who had dropped his sardonic grin for a look of devout contemplation, pushed a chair forward, and seated himself on a carved settle against the wall.

"Now, then," he said, "tell Clyde what you can; but the letter killeth."

He sank down, his hands hanging on the arm of the settle like the claws of a dead bird, his eyes fixed on Wyant's notebook with the obvious intention of detecting any attempt at a surreptitious sketch.

Wyant, nettled at this surveillance, and disturbed by the speculations which Doctor Lombard's strange household excited, sat motionless for a few minutes, staring first at the picture and then at the blank pages of the note-book. The thought that Doctor Lombard was enjoying his discomfiture at length roused him, and he began to write.

He was interrupted by a knock on the iron door. Doctor Lombard rose to unlock it, and his daughter entered.

She bowed hurriedly to Wyant, without looking at him.

"Father, had you forgotten that the man from Monte Amiato was to come back this morning with an answer about the bas-relief? He is here now; he says he can't wait."

"The devil!" cried her father impatiently. "Didn't you tell him—"

"Yes; but he says he can't come back. If you want to see him you must come now."

"Then you think there's a chance?—"

She nodded.

He turned and looked at Wyant, who was writing assiduously.

"You will stay here, Sybilla; I shall be back in a moment."

He hurried out, locking the door behind him.

Wyant had looked up, wondering if Miss Lombard would show any surprise at being locked in with him; but it was his turn to be surprised, for hardly had they heard the key withdrawn when she moved close to him, her small face pale and tumultuous.

"I arranged it—I must speak to you," she gasped. "He'll be back in five minutes."

Her courage seemed to fail, and she looked at him helplessly.

Wyant had a sense of stepping among explosives. He glanced about him at the dusky vaulted room, at the haunting smile of the strange picture overhead, and at the pink-and-white girl whispering of conspiracies in a voice meant to exchange platitudes with a curate.

"How can I help you?" he said with a rush of compassion.

"Oh, if you would! I never have a chance to speak to any one; it's so difficult—he watches me—he'll be back immediately."

"Try to tell me what I can do."

"I don't dare; I feel as if he were behind me." She turned away, fixing her eyes on the picture. A sound startled her. "There he comes, and I haven't spoken! It was my only chance; but it bewilders me so to be hurried."

"I don't hear any one," said Wyant, listening. "Try to tell me."

"How can I make you understand? It would take so long to explain." She drew a deep breath, and then with a plunge—"Will you come here again this afternoon—at about five?" she whispered.

"Come here again?"

"Yes—you can ask to see the picture,—make some excuse. He will come with you, of course; I will open the door for you—and—and lock you both in"—she gasped.

"Lock us in?"

"You see? You understand? It's the only way for me to leave the house—if I am ever to do it"—She drew another difficult breath. "The key will be returned—by a safe person—in half an hour,—perhaps sooner—"

She trembled so much that she was obliged to lean against the settle for support.

"Wyant looked at her steadily; he was very sorry for her.

"I can't, Miss Lombard," he said at length.

"You can't?"

"I'm sorry; I must seem cruel; but consider—"

He was stopped by the futility of the word: as well ask a hunted rabbit to pause in its dash for a hole!

Wyant took her hand; it was cold and nerveless.

"I will serve you in any way I can; but you must see that this way is impossible. Can't I talk to you again? Perhaps—"

"Oh," she cried, starting up, "there he comes!"

Doctor Lombard's step sounded in the passage.

Wyant held her fast. "Tell me one thing: he won't let you sell the picture?"

"No—hush!"

"Make no pledges for the future, then; promise me that."

"The future?"

"In case he should die: your father is an old man. You haven't promised?"

She shook her head.

"Don't, then; remember that."

She made no answer, and the key turned in the lock.

As he passed out of the house, its scowling cornice and facade of ravaged brick looked down on him with the startlingness of a strange face, seen momentarily in a crowd, and impressing itself on the brain as part of an inevitable future. Above the doorway, the marble hand reached out like the cry of an imprisoned anguish.

Wyant turned away impatiently.

"Rubbish!" he said to himself. "SHE isn't walled in; she can get out if she wants to."

CHAPTER IV

Wyant had any number of plans for coming to Miss Lombard's aid: he was elaborating the twentieth when, on the same afternoon, he stepped into the express train for Florence. By the time the train reached Certaldo he was convinced that, in thus hastening his departure, he had followed the only reasonable course; at Empoli, he began to reflect that the priest and the Levite had probably justified themselves in much the same manner.

A month later, after his return to England, he was unexpectedly relieved from these alternatives of extenuation and approval. A paragraph in the morning paper announced the sudden death of Doctor Lombard, the distinguished English dilettante who had long resided in Siena. Wyant's justification was complete. Our blindest impulses become evidence of perspicacity when they fall in with the course of events.

Wyant could now comfortably speculate on the particular complications from which his foresight had probably saved him. The climax was unexpectedly dramatic. Miss Lombard, on the brink of a step which, whatever its issue, would have burdened her with retrospective compunction, had been set free before her suitor's ardor could have had time to cool, and was now doubtless planning a life of domestic felicity on the proceeds of the Leonardo. One thing, however, struck

Wyant as odd—he saw no mention of the sale of the picture. He had scanned the papers for an immediate announcement of its transfer to one of the great museums; but presently concluding that Miss Lombard, out of filial piety, had wished to avoid an appearance of unseemly haste in the disposal of her treasure, he dismissed the matter from his mind. Other affairs happened to engage him; the months slipped by, and gradually the lady and the picture dwelt less vividly in his mind.

It was not till five or six years later, when chance took him again to Siena, that the recollection started from some inner fold of memory. He found himself, as it happened, at the head of Doctor Lombard's street, and glancing down that grim thoroughfare, caught an oblique glimpse of the doctor's house front, with the Dead Hand projecting above its threshold. The sight revived his interest, and that evening, over an admirable frittata, he questioned his landlady about Miss Lombard's marriage.

"The daughter of the English doctor? But she has never married, signore."

"Never married? What, then, became of Count Ottaviano?"

"For a long time he waited; but last year he married a noble lady of the Maremma."

"But what happened—why was the marriage broken?"

The landlady enacted a pantomime of baffled

interrogation.

"And Miss Lombard still lives in her father's house?"

"Yes, signore; she is still there."

"And the Leonardo—"

"The Leonardo, also, is still there."

The next day, as Wyant entered the House of the Dead Hand, he remembered Count Ottaviano's injunction to ring twice, and smiled mournfully to think that so much subtlety had been vain. But what could have prevented the marriage? If Doctor Lombard's death had been long delayed, time might have acted as a dissolvent, or the young lady's resolve have failed; but it seemed impossible that the white heat of ardor in which Wyant had left the lovers should have cooled in a few short weeks.

As he ascended the vaulted stairway the atmosphere of the place seemed a reply to his conjectures. The same numbing air fell on him, like an emanation from some persistent will-power, a something fierce and imminent which might reduce to impotence every impulse within its range. Wyant could almost fancy a hand on his shoulder, guiding him upward with the ironical intent of confronting him with the evidence of its work.

A strange servant opened the door, and he was presently introduced to the tapestried room, where, from their usual seats in the window, Mrs. Lombard and her daughter advanced to welcome him with faint ejaculations of surprise.

Both had grown oddly old, but in a dry, smooth way, as fruits might shrivel on a shelf instead of ripening on the tree. Mrs. Lombard was still knitting, and pausing now and then to warm her swollen hands above the brazier; and Miss Lombard, in rising, had laid aside a strip of needle-work which might have been the same on which Wyant had first seen her engaged.

Their visitor inquired discreetly how they had fared in the interval, and learned that they had thought of returning to England, but had somehow never done so.

"I am sorry not to see my aunts again," Mrs. Lombard said resignedly; "but Sybilla thinks it best that we should not go this year."

"Next year, perhaps," murmured Miss Lombard, in a voice which seemed to suggest that they had a great waste of time to fill.

She had returned to her seat, and sat bending over her work. Her hair enveloped her head in the same thick braids, but the rose color of her cheeks had turned to blotches of dull red, like some pigment which has darkened in drying.

"And Professor Clyde—is he well?" Mrs. Lombard asked affably; continuing, as her daughter raised a startled eye: "Surely, Sybilla, Mr. Wyant was the gentleman who was sent by Professor Clyde to see the Leonardo?"

Miss Lombard was silent, but Wyant hastened to assure the elder lady of his friend's well-being.

"Ah—perhaps, then, he will come back some day to Siena," she said, sighing. Wyant declared that it was more than likely; and there ensued a pause, which he presently broke by saying to Miss Lombard: "And you still have the picture?"

She raised her eyes and looked at him. "Should you like to see it?" she asked.

On his assenting, she rose, and extracting the same key from the same secret drawer, unlocked the door beneath the tapestry. They walked down the passage in silence, and she stood aside with a grave gesture, making Wyant pass before her into the room. Then she crossed over and drew the curtain back from the picture.

The light of the early afternoon poured full on it: its surface appeared to ripple and heave with a fluid splendor. The colors had lost none of their warmth, the outlines none of their pure precision; it seemed to Wyant like some magical flower which had burst suddenly from the mould of darkness and oblivion.

He turned to Miss Lombard with a movement of comprehension.

"Ah, I understand—you couldn't part with it, after all!" he cried.

"No—I couldn't part with it," she answered.

"It's too beautiful,—too beautiful,"—he assented.

"Too beautiful?" She turned on him with a curious stare.

"I have never thought it beautiful, you know."

He gave back the stare. "You have never—"

She shook her head. "It's not that. I hate it; I've always hated it. But he wouldn't let me—he will never let me now."

Wyant was startled by her use of the present tense. Her look surprised him, too: there was a strange fixity of resentment in her innocuous eye. Was it possible that she was laboring under some delusion? Or did the pronoun not refer to her father?

"You mean that Doctor Lombard did not wish you to part with the picture?"

"No—he prevented me; he will always prevent me."

There was another pause. "You promised him, then, before his death—"

"No; I promised nothing. He died too suddenly to make me." Her voice sank to a whisper. "I was free—perfectly free—or I thought I was till I tried."

"Till you tried?"

"To disobey him—to sell the picture. Then I found it was impossible. I tried again and again; but he was always in the room with me."

She glanced over her shoulder as though she had heard a step; and to Wyant, too, for a moment, the room seemed full of a third presence.

"And you can't"—he faltered, unconsciously dropping his voice to the pitch of hers.

She shook her head, gazing at him mystically. "I can't lock him out; I can never lock him out now. I told you I should never have another chance."

Wyant felt the chill of her words like a cold breath in his hair.

"Oh"—he groaned; but she cut him off with a grave gesture.

"It is too late," she said; "but you ought to have helped me that day."